THE RED SHOES MYSTERY

Book 2 in the Mayo Murder Series

DAVID PEARSON

***

Published by Booksbypearson ®
Dublin, Ireland

David Pearson is a prolific author of gripping Irish crime fiction.
For a complete list of all his titles, see the web site www.booksbypearson.com

Dedicated to all those who make their living writing compelling crime-fiction books.

Chapter One

It was high summer. Westport, on the Atlantic seaboard of Ireland, was enjoying a spell of hot, dry weather, with an area of high pressure firmly anchored above the country. It seemed that there were endless days of sunshine and temperatures in the high twenties Celsius. It was a welcome change from the very wet winter and spring the area had come through. The land was drying out nicely, giving the farmers the chance of a decent harvest.

All around the town tourists thronged the streets. The hotels were totally booked out; the bed and breakfast establishments were likewise booked, and even the Airbnb places were full, not to mention the various caravan and camping sites that were dotted around the rugged Atlantic coast.

Down at Bertra Beach, a long sandy spit of land reaching out into Clew Bay some 12km west of Westport, a small camping site housed just 10 static mobile homes and gave shelter to a few tents for mostly young people at busy times. The council had also provided a large parking area here overlooking the coast, with spaces marked out in white lines on the smooth black tarmacadam. By day, these parking places provided an excellent viewing point for visitors or parking for the hardier types that wanted to swim in the cold Atlantic Ocean, and they were also often used by people with camper vans who overnighted at the spot, enjoying the magnificent sunsets far out to the west.

At this time of year, people said that it never really got totally dark. Out to the west, the sky would eventually blacken at around 3 am, but at the same time, the first early signs of the new day appeared in the east, with a lightening overhead heralding the dawn.

It was at this time, approximately, that the strange events of that summer night began to develop. There was a French couple parked in a large, white camper van at one end of the parking area in front of the caravan park, and the occupants had gone to bed sometime after 11 pm. They had a busy day ahead of them, as they were planning to drive to Donegal to continue their tour of Ireland, and the west coast in particular.

They were awoken by a small number of loud bangs and a strange orange glow that filled their temporary dwelling, accompanied by a pungent smell of smoke and burning chemicals. On getting out of bed to investigate, the Frenchman pulled back the curtains to the side of his vehicle and looked out to see a car at the far end of the parking lot in flames. The man quickly found his mobile phone and dialled 112, reporting, in somewhat broken English, what he was looking at.

The call handler in Castlerea was patient, listening carefully to what the Frenchman was telling him and making sure to get the location of the incident recorded. When the call ended, he wasted no time in alerting the Fire Brigade in Westport, who were located in a modern facility on Leenane Road, where the duty officer urgently turned out two appliances and a crew of six to go to the scene. As a matter of course, the call centre also notified the Gardaí in Westport, where the night duty man listened with surprise to the story he was being told.

"Thanks for letting us know. I'm not sure where the patrol car is just now. They were out near Castlebar earlier, but I haven't spoken to them in a while. I'll see if I can get them on the radio and ask them to stop by Bertra," the night sergeant in Westport said.

"Grand, so. Good night, Sergeant," the call handler replied.

After a few attempts, the sergeant got on the radio and managed to raise the two uniformed officers in the squad car.

"We've had a report of a vehicle on fire out at Bertra strand, Jim. Where are you at the moment?"

"We're over near Carrowbeg, Sarge. There was some report of a break-in at one of the pubs here, but we couldn't find any evidence of anything amiss. Do you want us to go to Bertra? All the drama will probably be over by the time we get there. It's a good half-hour from here."

"Are you finished where you are, Jim?"

"Yes. As I said, nothing untoward here."

"Well then, maybe you should attend. I haven't much information about it. Apparently, a Frenchman reported it to the Fire Brigade, and they were off to see what's what. So, you'd better put in an appearance, even if, as you say, it's all over by the time you get there. OK, Jim?"

"Yes, OK, Sarge. Show us attending."

* * *

The two red fire engines drove out in convoy towards Bertra Beach. They had their blue lights on, but there was no need for sirens, as there was virtually no traffic on the road at that hour of the morning. It took them just 12 minutes to make the journey, and when they arrived, the vehicle was still burning brightly, emitting thick black smoke, although there wasn't much left of the upper part of the car by this time. Paddy O'Leary, the lead fireman, wasted no time in getting his crew kitted up, and within a few minutes, they were hosing down the conflagration using water stored in the fire tenders. A small crowd from the caravan site had gathered to observe the spectacle, and O'Leary had to ask them to stand well back, in case the car's petrol tank exploded. He was well used to dealing with vehicle fires and recognized the danger that they posed.

After 20 minutes, the smouldering hulk of what had been Toyota saloon was all that was left. It was still very hot, giving off steam from the water that had been used to douse the fire, but it was nevertheless extinguished. A putrid stench hung in the air from the rubber and plastic that had been consumed by the flames. When O'Leary was happy that the burnt-out wreck posed no danger, he approached it, and using a crowbar from the toolbox in his own vehicle, he pulled open the front passenger door. He looked inside and recoiled quickly from the sight before him.

O'Leary stood away from the car with his back to it and called Westport Garda station on his mobile phone.

"Sergeant. This is Paddy O'Leary, lead fireman. I'm out at Bertra Beach with that vehicle fire that was reported earlier. You'd better get someone senior out to me as soon as you can."

"Oh, right, Paddy. What's the problem?"

"The problem is that there's a dead body in the car!"

Chapter Two

DI Martin O'Shea was used to rising early, but not at 4:30 am. He answered his phone tentatively, hoping that his wife, Angela, asleep beside him in their marital bed, had not been disturbed.

"Yes," he whispered, easing himself out of bed and walking towards the en-suite bathroom. Once inside, he closed the door quietly.

The sergeant at Westport gave O'Shea the details of the incident at Bertra and asked O'Shea if he could attend.

"Yes, OK, Sergeant. I'll go on out there now, but I doubt if there's much I can do at this hour of the night. Can you alert the pathologist and make sure there are some uniforms there to preserve the scene."

"Yes, of course, sir. I'll get on it straight away."

O'Shea crept back into the bedroom and put on his clothes as quietly as possible, but as he was tying the knot in his tie, Angela stirred and asked in a drowsy voice, "What time is it? Where are you going?"

"Sorry, love. I have to go out. Some nonsense going on out at Bertra. I'll call you when I know what's what."

"OK, love. Be careful," and she turned over and went back to sleep.

* * *

By the time Martin O'Shea got to the crime scene, it was fully bright. It was a clear, sunny morning. The good weather seemed set to continue. The two fire appliances were still there, with the crew tidying up the last of their equipment. Two uniformed Gardaí stood in front of a line of blue and white scene-of-crime plastic tape that had been anchored by three yellow Garda traffic cones that were carried in the boot of the police car. O'Shea approached the nearest Garda.

"Morning, Jim. What's the story here, then?" O'Shea said to the young man.

"Good morning, sir. This was called in by one of the visitors in a camper van in the small hours. I have his details. He doesn't know about the body."

"Who found it, then?"

"Oh, it was the fire chief, sir. The one with the white helmet. He's over there by the tender."

"Thanks. Has anyone else been here?" O'Shea said.

"No, sir. Just us and the firemen. There were a few rubberneckers from the camp site, but we got rid of them. None of them knows about the person in the car, sir."

"Good. Well done. Do you know if the pathologist is on the way?"

"Yes, sir. I had a call from Dr Mulhall. She said she'd be here in around and hour and a half."

"Great. OK. I'm going to talk to the fire crew. Are you OK with hanging on here and preserving the scene for a while?" O'Shea said.

"Yes, sir. The sarge said he'll get some replacements out to us as soon as the morning shift shows up. But we're grand till then."

O'Shea walked over to where Paddy O'Leary was standing, talking to one of his men. O'Shea knew the man from previous encounters, although none had been quite so gruesome as this one.

"Good morning, Paddy. This is a rum do. What's the story?" O'Shea said.

"Morning, Inspector. Yes, not a pretty sight," O'Leary said, gesturing towards the burnt-out hulk of the car. The two men walked over slowly to the passenger's side of the charred shell, and O'Leary pointed inside.

"We thought at first it was just a car fire. We get a few of those, but not usually in as scenic a spot as this. They're usually on rough ground at the back of an industrial estate or something. So, we did the usual. Extinguished the blaze, staying well back until it was almost out in case it exploded. Then I moved in and nearly had a heart attack. I'm not the better of it yet."

O'Shea moved in closer to the car and could see the badly burnt remains of a person, still propped up by the metal frame of the seat in which it had been seated. All of the person's hair was gone, and the skin on the upper torso was blackened and blistered. Some of the clothes had melted, too, and stuck to what was left of the body. But the last 20cm of both the individual's legs were still intact, as well as the red, flat shoes she had been wearing.

"Cripes, how come the feet survived, Paddy?"

"The fire appears to have started in the back of the car, and it spread upwards and forwards, but the passenger's foot well remained relatively cool. As you can see, it's a woman or a girl," O'Leary said.

"No sign of the driver, I suppose?" O'Shea said.

"No. He definitely wasn't in the car when it went up. And there's been accelerant used, too. Probably petrol, but there's a lot of that all around, so you'll need to get your forensic people to confirm."

"Yes, there on their way, I think. Do you know if the seat belt was fastened on the passenger side?"

"No, it wasn't. The buckle would still be in the holder if it had been, even though the belt itself has burnt away."

"Hmm .. so, if she'd been alert, she could have got out," O'Shea said.

"I guess. But I'm no expert," the senior fireman said.

"Can you tell me anything else, Paddy?"

O'Leary though for a moment before replying.

"Well, it's a diesel-fuelled car. Is that any help? We should be able to get the VIN number off it when it cools down. That might help you identify the owner, though it could be stolen. Most burnt-out cars we come across are. There's no sign of the container. They usually throw the can back into the vehicle as it burns, so it's destroyed along with any fingerprints, but not in this case."

"What about a registration number?" O'Shea said.

"Sorry. The plates were plastic. Both burnt beyond

recognition, as were the tax disk and insurance details from the windscreen."

"OK, Paddy. I'd better let you get away. Thanks for your help."

"No problem, Inspector. I'll have it all written up and emailed to you as soon as I can."

"Thanks, Paddy. Catch you later."

O'Shea then walked the length of the car park to where the camper van with the visitors who had initially reported the fire was parked. He knocked on the door.

After just a couple of seconds, the door swung outwards, and a thin, bearded man who was, O'Shea guessed, in his mid-thirties, wearing jeans and a polo shirt, stood in the doorway.

"Good morning, sir. My name is Detective Inspector Martin O'Shea. I understand that you were the person who reported the fire," O'Shea said, nodding back over his shoulder in the direction of the wreck.

"Yes, that's correct," the man said in a distinctly foreign accent.

"I wonder if I could ask you a few questions." O'Shea said.

"Yes, of course. Won't you come in please," the man said, reversing back into the van. O'Shea climbed the two steps up into the accommodation, which was surprisingly spacious and in very good order.

"I am Vittoire Durand, and this is my wife, Celine," the man said, gesturing towards a very petite blonde woman seated at the table that dissected the available floor space. "Would you like a coffee, Inspector? I'm afraid we don't have any tea," Durand said.

"No, thanks, Monsieur Durand, I'm fine," O'Shea said, though in truth, he could have done with some refreshment.

"Please, call me Vittoire. How can we help?"

"If you could just tell me what you saw or heard, Vittoire?"

"Well, we were asleep, of course. We sleep very well, and this is a nice peaceful place, so there is nothing to disturb us. I was awoken by some noise outside – a sort of crackling and a few small bangs. I could also see an orange glow coming through the windows. So, I got up and looked out, and I saw the burning car. I woke Celine. We didn't want to go near it in case it could blow up, so I just phoned 112 and reported it. Did I do the right thing, Inspector?"

"Oh, yes, of course. But may I ask, did either of you see anyone near the car or running away?"

Durand looked at his wife and shrugged.

"No, we didn't. Why? Do you think there was someone in the car?"

"Can you remember if the car was there when you went to bed last night, Vittoire?" O'Shea said.

"No. It wasn't. I went to fill our water container up at the camp site at around 10:30 pm, and we were the only vehicle here at that time."

"So, you don't know when it arrived then?"

"No. I'm sorry. Does this happen often here, Inspector?"

"No. Not at all. It's very rare, in fact, I don't think there has ever been a vehicle fire here before. But I have to tell you both, I'm afraid there was a body found inside the wreck. It was a young woman, and of course, she didn't survive."

Durand staggered back and landed on the seat beside his wife.

"Oh, *mon Dieu*. That's terrible. Do you know who she is?"

"No, not as yet. But may I ask again, are you certain you didn't hear or see anything before the fire woke you up?"

"No, definitely not. I'm sorry."

"Never mind, Vittoire. Don't worry. But if I could ask you to stop by the police station in Westport later before you leave the area to make a statement. Would that be all right?"

"Yes, of course. We can find it with the sat nav."

"Thanks. I'll leave you alone now, then. And don't let this spoil your holiday. It's a very unusual event. Where are you going next?" O'Shea said.

"Donegal, if that's OK?"

"Yes, of course. It's very beautiful. Enjoy it, and try not to think about what has happened here."

"Thank you, Inspector."

Chapter Three

Detective Sergeant Deirdre Maguire arrived in Westport Garda station at her usual time of 8:30 am. As she breezed in through the reception area, the desk sergeant caught her attention.

"I wouldn't get too cosy, Deirdre if I were you. The DI is way out at Bertra, and he's been looking for you," the desk sergeant said.

"Oh. What's the story, Liam?" Maguire said.

"Something about a burnt-out car. But I think he's after finding a body inside it."

"Blooming hell! When was this?"

"He's been out there since first light. Will you go out and see what gives?"

"Yes, of course, and I'd better bring some coffee for him too. He'll be like a bear with a sore head."

Liam smiled as Maguire turned on her heel and left again.

* * *

By the time Maguire arrived out at Bertra, armed with four take-away coffees in insulated mugs and several doughnuts, the place was a hive of activity. The forensic team had arrived and put up a protective tent around the front of the torched car, and Dr Mulhall's vehicle was parked nearby, although there was no sign of the woman herself. Maguire assumed she was inside the tent seeing the deceased.

"Morning, boss. I brought some coffee and a few buns," Maguire said.

"Morning, Deirdre. The lads will be very grateful, I'm sure," he said, reaching out and taking a cup for himself and drinking a few mouthfuls.

"So, what's the story, boss?" Maguire said.

O'Shea brought his sergeant up to speed between mouthfuls of doughnut and the very welcome hot drink. The other Gardaí came across and helped themselves to the refreshments too, as Maguire leaned back against the side of her car, taking in the scene.

"Any ID on the woman?" Maguire asked.

"No. Nothing. Just her shoes left. The rest of her and her clothes are destroyed. But there's a few things that don't really add up," O'Shea said.

"Oh. Such as?"

"Well, her seat belt wasn't fastened, so why didn't she get out when the car caught fire? And there's no sign of the driver, and of course, no chance of any fingerprint evidence either."

"Has the doc anything useful to say?" Maguire said.

"Not yet. I haven't spoken to her since she arrived. She's been busy."

Just then, on cue, as it were, Dr Mulhall stepped out of

the white tent and removed her face mask, hood and gloves. Mulhall was in her late forties. She was tall with a trim figure and nicely styled brown hair that fell to her shoulders. O'Shea had met her a number of times previously and had always found her to be extremely efficient, even if her sense of humour could, at times, be rather dark.

"Inspector, Sergeant. Nice day for it. She's in a bit of a state though, isn't she?" Mulhall said.

"You could say that all right," O'Shea responded, "so, what can you tell us so far, doc?"

"Not a whole lot. A young woman, possibly in her twenties or early thirties. Not overweight. Size five shoes, so probably around five foot four to five foot seven in height, but that's just a guesstimate. I'll be able to tell you a lot more when I do the post-mortem."

"And what about the usual, Doc?" Maguire said.

"Oh, you mean, what did she die of and how long ago? Well, I'd say the cause of death is pretty obvious. As to the time, I'd say about twenty minutes before you received the notification of the fire. But again, I'll know more when I've done the post-mortem."

"When will you get to it, doc?" O'Shea asked.

"It's not going to be easy to get her out of there without causing a lot more damage. The plastic seat coverings have melted and stuck to her. But all being well, we should have her back in Castlebar by lunchtime, so shall we say 3 pm?"

"Yes, thanks. We'll see you there."

Dr Mulhall walked back to the white tent and issued instructions to her assistants. She then got back into her vehicle and drove off towards Westport.

"What now, boss?" Maguire said, draining the last of her coffee.

"I'm going to stay here and talk to some of the residents of the caravan site. I'd like you to go back to the station and start looking into the missing persons who match the description Mulhall gave us. And where the hell are forensics? They should be her by now."

"I'll chase them up. They'll probably want to get the car back to the station, and I'm sure the council won't want it here any longer than absolutely necessary, either. Is that OK with you, boss?"

"Yes, no problem, as long as they do a decent search of the area first before they move it."

"OK. I'll see to it. I should be back at the ranch in about twenty minutes. Keep in touch," Maguire said.

"OK. See ya."

On the drive back to Westport, Maguire used the hands-free system in her car to contact the forensic team lead on her phone.

"Hi, Kevin. It's Deirdre Maguire. The inspector is wondering when you'll be able to get out to Bertra. He's getting a bit impatient."

"Oh, hello, Sergeant. We're on our way out now. I understand we may need a tow truck, too. Is that right?"

"Yes, but the body hasn't been removed yet, so that won't be for another hour or so. But you can get started on the area around the car for any evidence that may have been left behind."

"OK, right. We should be there is about ten minutes."

"Great. Talk soon."

Chapter Four

When DS Maguire got back to Westport Garda station, she summoned the remainder of her team into DI O'Shea's office. Detective Garda Liam Staunton was a keen young officer who was studying for his sergeant's exams. He was tall and thin, with a mop of fair, curly hair, and had proved very adept at handling a few quite tricky situations in the past. Maguire liked him for his pragmatic and professional approach to policing and trusted him implicitly.

Detective Garda Agnes Gallagher was another young officer who had, in the past year, graduated from being in uniform to her current status as a plain clothes detective. She was a pretty woman in her mid-twenties and showed a lot of promise, too. During a nasty incident the previous year when her parents had been held hostage by a killer, she had acted cleverly to ensure that evidence was protected and no harm came to her folks without parting with anything of value to the criminal.

Maguire outlined the events of the morning to the two

of them and went on to set up a number of tasks for them both.

"Liam, can you start working on missing persons? We're looking for a woman in her late twenties, possibly around five-six tall, or thereabouts, with any connection to anyone who drives a Toyota Avensis."

"Is that it? No description of what she was wearing or her identity?"

"I'm afraid not, Liam. If you'd seen the body, you'd understand. She's destroyed, but wait, she was wearing red shoes," Maguire said.

"Oh, OK, sorry, boss. Yes. I'll get onto it right away, but it's not a whole lot to go on," Staunton said.

"Just do what you can, Liam. Agnes, I'd like you to concentrate on the car. Forensics will have a VIN number by now. Give Kevin Molloy a call-out at the scene and get the number. Then, I get busy finding registration details for the car and the recorded keeper. We know it is, or was, a Toyota Avensis. The original model, so it's not new or nearly new. And while that's going on, see if there's any CCTV anywhere on the road out to Bertra that might have captured the vehicle going there last night. It was sometime between 11 pm and 3 am, according to the man who called it in. By the way, he's coming in to make a statement, so let them know at the front desk and ask them to call me when he arrives."

"OK, boss. Anything else?" Gallagher asked.

"No, not now

. But keep me updated with anything relevant as the day goes on. I'll be going across for the post-mortem later on. Dr Mulhall said around three o'clock."

* * *

Back at Bertra, DI O'Shea was having no luck at all with the residents of the caravan park. No one had seen anything in any way helpful. They were more interested in peppering him with questions than providing any information of value to him, and he was getting quite frustrated.

After a wasted hour, he made his way back to where the car was located. The body of the passenger had now been removed, and the forensic team were busy exploring all around the area and of course, focusing on the vehicle itself.

"Hi, Kevin. Anything interesting?" O'Shea said.

"A few things, sir. Fires are very strange. I mean, who would have thought that some paperwork in the glove box would survive," Kevin said, holding up a plastic evidence bag. "And I gave the VIN number to your Agnes a while back. She rang me and asked for it."

"Anything else?"

"Maybe. One of the lads found an empty red plastic petrol can down at the shore. It could just be crap that's washed in, but it might be the container the arsonist used. We have it secured in any case."

"The driver obviously made off once he had set the fire. Is there any sign of another vehicle having been here apart from the camper van?" O'Shea said.

"No, I'm afraid not. This surface doesn't hold tyre tracks at all. It's too smooth. But I know what you mean. Did no one up at the caravan park see or hear anything?"

O'Shea rolled his eyes.

"Nothing. Useless lot. You'd think someone would have seen or heard something, but not a whisper. Or maybe they just don't want to get involved. Who knows. Have you much more to do here, Kevin?"

"Nah. I want to get the car lifted and brought back in to the station. The engine is more or less intact, apart from the wiring, so the oil will still be in there. We might be able to get something from that, or maybe get a print off the dipstick or washer bottle lid."

"Right. Well, let me know later if there's any good news, won't you?"

"Yes, of course."

* * *

The Frenchman came into the Garda station mid-way through the morning. Maguire met him and asked him again what he had seen, but he had little to add to his earlier account. He completed a written statement and left his contact details in France, saying that he would be touring Ireland for the next four days, but after that, he would return home and could be contacted in France if needed.

Maguire felt that he would be of little further use to them, although he had helped to pinpoint the time of the incident.

Three o'clock came around quickly, with no major developments amongst the team. O'Shea and Maguire drove along the R309, skirting Islandeady and on through Dernagro to Mayo University Hospital in Castlebar. It was once again a fine Summer's Day, and by now, the temperature had reached an unusually high 25 degrees. They turned in opposite the Royal Hotel and parked at the rear of the main hospital building where the mortuary was located.

Chapter Five

Maguire didn't like post-mortems. The clinical atmosphere, the strong smell of disinfectant, and of course, the remains itself, combined to make her nauseous and uncomfortable. This one was worse than most.

Maguire and O'Shea positioned themselves in a viewing gallery above the gurney where the body of the dead woman was laid out. The pathologist and her team had managed to more or less straighten out the woman's limbs, but the extensive burning on the body, with the blackened and blistered skin was hideous. There was a microphone suspended over the corpse that picked up Dr Mulhall's commentary and relayed it to the viewing gallery. Mulhall approached the dead woman and circled the shiny aluminium table as she started to inspect the remains.

"The body of a woman is estimated to be in her twenties. Severely burnt in a vehicle fire, with only the last 30 centimetres of her legs left unscathed," Mulhall said as she walked around the table.

"Estimated weight at the time of death 115 pounds or 51 kilogrammes, approximately. Height when alive in the region of 5 foot 6 inches or 1.7 metres."

Mulhall then moved in closer to the woman and pulled down a strong inspection lamp that was suspended over the examination table.

"Very extensive burning to the head and upper torso, with much of the outer layers of skin consumed. The fire did less damage as we moved down the body, but all of her head and body hair has gone. The remains of her clothing has been removed and is being forensically examined. Early indications are that she may have been fair-haired, based on some stray hairs found on her jacket collar, which paradoxically seems to have avoided the worst of the fire."

Mulhall then turned her attention to the woman's head. Using gloved hands, she gently rotated the head through about 45 degrees and zoned in on the side of the skull on the woman's right-hand side. Mulhall turned to her assistant, who was shadowing her around and asked for a magnifying glass.

She switched on the ring of LED lights around the edge of the glass and moved in close to the dead woman's head.

"There are indications of blunt force trauma to the side of the head here," she said, gently exploring the cadaver.

O'Shea was prompted to ask the doctor about her findings.

"Is there any indication of what might have caused that injury, Doctor?"

"Give me a minute, Inspector," she said as she continued to examine the site of the impact. Mulhall took a rather gruesome-looking instrument from her assistant and probed further into the wound.

"OK. This is just a guess for now, but I'd say it might have been a hammer. It's circular, and it was heavy, so maybe something like a domestic hammer would have done it. Nasty."

"Do you think it could have killed her, Doctor?" Maguire asked.

"I'll know for sure when we get into her lungs, but I'd say it could easily have seen her off. That's quite a soft part of the head, and any severe injury there can often be fatal."

O'Shea decided they had had enough for now.

"OK. Well, I think we'll leave you to it, Doctor. I'd like to talk to the forensic team while you finish up here. How long more will you be?" O'Shea said.

"About another hour, Inspector, give or take."

"OK. Well, I might see you before you're done. Thanks."

As Maguire left the mortuary, she bumped into DI O'Shea.

They made their way together to the forensic laboratory which was situated in another area of the hospital complex. When they got there, they found Kevin Molloy at his bench with fragments of the deceased's clothing spread out in front of him and a pair of flat red shoes. Kevin pointed to the shoes.

"Shoes," he said, rather unnecessarily. "Interesting," he went on.

Maguire moved over in front of the two red shoes that had, remarkably, escaped the inferno in the car completely.

"What can you tell us about these then, Kevin?"

"They're Polish, as in from Poland. The brand name is

stencilled on the insole. Its Rylko. I looked up their website, and they have a wide range of women's shoes, and they aren't cheap."

"What sort of money?" Maguire asked.

"In and around €100 a pair," the young man replied.

"You obviously haven't bought any ladies shoes lately, Kevin. €100 isn't supermarket prices, but it's not exactly Jimmy Choo either. Very middle of the road. So, our victim could be Eastern European. Is that what you're thinking?"

"Obviously, it's not conclusive. But I don't think that brand is carried by any Irish shops. I had a look on the web. Certainly not in these parts, in any case."

It was O'Shea's turn to speak up.

"What about the rest of her clobber, Kevin?"

"Ah, it's all in bits, Inspector. I only have fragments. I'll examine it all again carefully but don't get your hopes up. I'll see if I can recover any labels from anything, but it's all been more or less destroyed."

"Is there any hope of identifying the victim at all then?" O'Shea asked.

Molloy just shrugged and looked rather sorrowfully at the two detectives.

"OK. Thanks, Kevin. Come on, Deirdre. Let's get back to the station."

As they were making their way towards the door, Dr Mulhall called to them.

"Have you got a moment, Inspector?" she said.

"Yes, of course. What is it," O'Shea replied.

"It's just that I've examined the major organs of the victim now, and there's something odd. There's no smoke, well hardly any, in her lungs."

"Meaning?" O'Shea said.

"Well, it's difficult to be certain, but obviously, she was dead before the fire took hold. But it could also be that she was killed elsewhere and transported post mortem to the car park."

"Was it the blow to the head that did it?"

"Yes, I'd say so, and that makes sense because there isn't really enough room to swing a hammer with enough force to kill someone inside a car."

"Is there any way of confirming your suspicions, Doctor?"

"Not unless you can find the original murder site. There'll be a lot of blood all over it, for sure."

"OK. Well, thanks, I think! If anything else occurs, give us a shout."

Chapter Six

It was late afternoon when O'Shea and Maguire got back to the station. O'Shea wanted to get the team together, so he asked Maguire to set it up while he went off to get a mug of tea for both of them.

Detective Garda Liam Staunton and Detective Garda Agnes Gallagher were seated in the open plan when O'Shea and Maguire joined them. O'Shea began the conversation.

"Thanks, everyone. As you know, we have a dead girl that was discovered out at Bertra beach in a burnt-out car. We've just come back from the post-mortem. There's very little evidence available, but Kevin did manage to identify a pair of red shoes that seem to have come from Poland, or at least were made there. We also know that the car was a Toyota Avensis, and apparently, it was black in colour," O'Shea said.

"Isn't that an unusual colour for one of those?" Staunton asked.

Deirdre Maguire responded.

"Yes, it is, Liam. Most of those were either silver or a sort of gold colour. So, that gives us a lead of sorts. Could you do a trawl of the car sales websites and see if you can find a black Avensis for sale anytime over the past six months? The fire chief said it had a diesel engine, so that might help a bit."

"Yes, sure, Sarge. Do we have the registration number?" Staunton asked.

"No, I'm afraid not. But we can get the VIN number if that helps," Maguire said.

Agnes Gallagher then asked, "What about the shoes?"

Again, Maguire took the lead.

"Good question, Agnes. Can you contact all the places that sell women's shoes here and in Castlebar and see if they stock Rylko shoes? If you draw a blank, extend the search to Sligo and Galway. And while you're at it, can you follow up on missing persons? Somebody must know who this lassie is."

"Yes, right, Sarge."

O'Shea decided to wrap up the meeting.

"OK, folks. Let's leave it at that for tonight. Get busy in the morning with these various tasks, and if anything breaks, come back to me or Deirdre immediately. Thanks," O'Shea said.

As the group broke up and prepared to leave the station for the evening, Maguire said to her boss, "Didn't Paddy O'Leary, the fireman, say that there was some paperwork in the glove box of the car that somehow survived?"

"Did he? Well, maybe you could follow that up and see if there's anything of interest, but knowing our luck, it will just be the owner's handbook."

"I'll call him now and see if he has anything."

"Right. I'm heading home. Catch you tomorrow."

"Yeah, see ya."

* * *

"Hi, Paddy. It's Deirdre Maguire here. Do I remember correctly that you said there was some paperwork in that burnt-out Toyota that didn't get destroyed in the fire?"

"Yes, there was. Let me see. I have it somewhere here. Do you want me to send it over?" O'Leary said.

"Yes, please, Paddy."

"OK. I'll get one of the lads to drop it off on the way home."

"Thanks."

"Is there any news on who the girl is or was?"

"No, I'm afraid not. She might have been an Eastern European, but we can't be sure. You haven't heard anything, I suppose?"

"No, sorry. Look, I'd better get going. I'll have that stuff over to you in about half an hour. Bye."

"Bye, Paddy, and thanks."

Maguire decided to hang around for the contents of the glove box to be left in at Westport Garda station. There was no obvious movement on the case, and she knew that Martin O'Shea and more importantly, his boss, Superintendent Derry O'Connell, were probably getting restless.

Twenty minutes later, the desk sergeant called Maguire and told her that a package had been left by one of the town's firemen for her. She thanked the man and went downstairs to collect it. When she got back to her desk, she opened the plastic evidence bag using vinyl gloves and spread the contents out. There was, as expected, the owner's manual for a Toyota Avensis, a service booklet; the vehicles NCT certificate, now long expired, and a few other miscellaneous bits of paper. But stuck to the outside of the service booklet, which had no recent stamps, there was a receipt from a local garage for diesel and petrol, amounting to €37.40c. It was dated the day before the fire. The diesel had come to €30, and the petrol accounted for the balance, making, Maguire calculated roughly, enough for approximately four litres of petrol. Just enough to fill the type of can that had been found on the beach.

Maguire remembered the red petrol container that the firemen had found. She tried to call Paddy O'Leary back again, but he had gone off duty. She made a mental note to follow up with him the next day. In the meantime, she studied the receipt carefully, and although it was a little faded, she could make out the name of the garage that had issued it. It was from a large Circle K place out on Castlebar road, and Maguire decided to pay them a visit.

"But why keep the receipt if you're going to burn the car? That doesn't make any sense," she said to herself.

Maguire packed her things and left the station to go back to Castlebar, where she lived in a modern apartment near the town centre. She was uneasy. This case was mystifying her. Who was this foreign girl who had ended up so brutally murdered if, indeed, she was foreign at all? Why would anyone do such a thing? Maybe the girl had something on someone particularly nasty, or maybe it was some kind of chaotic lover's tiff gone badly wrong. She didn't know, and she didn't like not knowing.

She decided to give Eoin McNally a call. Eoin was a sort of boyfriend who worked for the large insurance company that had located itself in the county, and provided motor and house insurance to the entire country. Maguire would have liked to have more of a relationship with him, but somehow, her work always seemed to get in the way. Eoin was a claims investigator for the company and was often employed validating some of the larger claims to see that they were *bona fide*.

"Hi, Eoin, it's me, Deirdre," she said when he answered the phone.

"Hi, Deirdre. How's things?"

"Awful, really. I need cheering up. Are you free?"

"Eh, yes, sure. I'm still at work, but I can leave shortly. What do you want to do?"

"I don't know. Maybe you could just call around when you're done? I'll be home in fifteen minutes myself, and we could take it from there."

"Yes, OK. Have you eaten?" McNally asked.

"No, but I'm not that hungry anyway. See you in a while. OK?"

"Yes, see you."

McNally didn't know what was wrong with his friend, but there was obviously something bothering her. They didn't discuss their work a lot when they were together, but he knew enough to read the signals, and something was very obviously getting to her on this occasion.

Chapter Seven

McNally arrived at Deirdre Maguire's apartment half an hour after they had finished their phone call. He had been home and was now casually dressed in smart chinos and a navy polo shirt. Maguire let him in.

"Hi, Eoin. Thanks for coming around. Good to see you," and she moved in, taking him in her arms and giving him a very welcoming kiss. When they disengaged, he said, "Nice to see you too. What would you like to do?"

"Can we go for a drive? Do you mind?"

"'Course not. Where do you want to go?"

"Take me on a mystery tour," she said, smiling.

"OK. Get your jacket. Let's go."

McNally held the passenger door of his black Audi open for Maguire and closed it gently when she was seated inside, making sure not to catch any of her clothing.

When he got into the car himself, he said, "Why don't we drive up to Ballina? We can go the back way via Pontoon and Crossmolina. It will be nice up there this evening, and if your appetite has returned, we can get some grub in Ballina. How does that sound?"

"Perfect. Just right. Can we stop up Loch Conn and take a stroll down by the lake? I need to clear my head."

"Sounds like a plan," he said and started the car.

When they were underway, McNally ventured an enquiry of his companion.

"Is everything OK, Deirdre? You're very quiet," he said.

"Sorry, yes, I'm OK now, thanks. The case we're working on has me demented, though. Do you mind if I dump on you a bit?"

"No, of course not, And as I think you know, it will go no further."

Maguire told McNally about the discovery of the dead girl in the car at Bertra, giving him as much detail as she knew herself about the matter.

"We can't even trace the car, for God's sake! It's very frustrating."

"I might be able to help with that. We have access to loads of databases on cars in the job. I think we can get even more information than the Gardaí for some reason. Have you a registration number?" McNally said.

"No, but I have the vin. Would that be any use?"

"Definitely. You can give it to me later, and I'll see what I can find tomorrow morning for you. How's that?"

"That would be terrific. You don't have a database of Eastern European girls that wear expensive red shoes too, by any chance?"

McNally smiled. "I'm afraid not, love."

By this time, they had arrived at Massbrook. McNally

had been right. It was a lovely evening with a gentle breeze just tickling the surface of Loch Conn, creating soft ripples on the water. They got out and found a path down by the lake. The sound of the little waves lapping at the shore soothed Maguire's nerves as they strolled along hand in hand in companionable silence. When they got to where the narrow path turned back up towards the road, McNally stopped and took Maguire in his arms.

"Now it's my turn, Deirdre. Can I ask you something?"

"Of course!" She wondered what was coming.

"We get along pretty well together, don't we?" McNally said.

"We do," Maguire said cautiously.

"I'm just wondering where our relationship is going, that's all."

"Where would you like it to go, Eoin?"

"Hmph. Ever the policewoman!" he said, smiling. "I'm getting very fond of you, Deirdre. I'd like to be more a part of your life, but maybe you don't want that. I find it hard to read you," he said, looking into her eyes for clues.

"Oh, I'm sorry. That's the cop in me. We are trained not to give anything away, most of the time. But I know what you mean. I'm fond of you too, and I'd like us to be closer, but what about my job and all? I have to keep much of my independence. But I enjoy being with you, especially after dark," she said with a cheeky grin.

They embraced warmly for quite some time, standing at the edge of the lake, lost in each other, all thoughts of burnt-out cars and red shoes gone from Maguire's consciousness, for now at least.

* * *

When they got back into the car to continue the drive to Ballina, things between them had definitely changed. Both of them could sense it. They were closer, and that strange form of electricity, or whatever it is, that flows between two lovers, was there in spades.

McNally navigated through the narrow streets of Ballina till he arrived outside Dillon's bar and restaurant, close to the River Moy.

"I hope you're hungry," he said.

"Yes, I am now. Thanks, Eoin," Maguire said, leaning over and giving him a quick kiss on the cheek.

"Great. Let's eat!"

* * *

When they had finished a delicious meal at the restaurant, they set off back towards Castlebar. This time, McNally took the more direct route via Foxford, and just half an hour later, he was pulling up outside Maguire's apartment.

"I hope you're not in a hurry to get home, Eoin," Maguire said.

McNally smiled, and they both got out of the car, going indoors together.

The two of them spent a warm and intimate night in Maguire's bed, consummating their new relationship more than once. At 7:30 am, they both rose and although they hadn't had a great deal of sleep, they both had a definite spring in their steps.

Maguire made them a decent breakfast, and afterwards, they set off separately to go to work. As they parted outside Maguire's place, she said, "I'll see you soon, Mr McNally. Very soon."

Chapter Eight

Maguire was seated at her desk in the Garda station, nursing a cup of coffee. It was barely 10 a.m. when her desk phone rang. She picked up the receiver, giving the usual greeting, "Detective Sergeant Maguire."

"Hi. It's me," McNally said.

"Oh, hi, Eoin. Everything OK?"

"Yes, sure, no problem. I just thought I'd call you to get the VIN number of the car we were talking about."

"Oh, right. Sure. Hang on a minute, I have it here somewhere."

Maguire thumbed through her notebook to find the right page.

"Yes, here it is. Have you got a pen?" she said.

"Yes, fire ahead."

"It's S-B-1-6-4-D-B-N-0-0-E-0-4-4-7-5-1. Did you get that OK?"

"Yep! I'll see what I can find and get back to you in a while. Everything OK?" McNally said.

"Yes, thanks. More than OK. Now, go on and do some detecting for me!"

Maguire got up from her desk and went in search of DI O'Shea. He was in his office, absorbed in paperwork.

"Hi, boss. Can I disturb you?"

"Yes, of course, Deirdre. Come in. Take a seat. I'm glad of the break, really. This stuff is doing my head in. What's on your mind?"

"I was thinking. The woman in the car could well be Eastern European, right?" Maguire said.

"Possibly, yes, why?"

"Well, many of those people are employed in the hospitality sector. Why don't we get Liam and Agnes to do a trawl of the hotels, restaurants, and bars here in town to see if anyone knows anything?"

"Hmm.. not a bad idea. Get them to bring a picture of the shoes with them too, but not with her legs still in them. Get one from forensics showing the label. It just might ring a bell with someone."

"Right, I'll go and set that up. Have you anything new?"

"Nope, nothing. I'm still hoping someone will come forward with a missing person's report. But we can't hang around waiting for that," O'Shea said.

"I might have something more on the car a bit later. Eoin is doing some digging for me. He says he has access to stuff we can only dream of."

"OK, but be careful with that. He's not one of us."

"I will, boss, don't worry. He's very discreet."

* * *

Maguire briefed Agnes Gallagher and Liam Staunton.

"Start here in Westport. Hopefully, you'll get some information from some of the other immigrants. Take a very soft approach. They can be sensitive to police enquiries. The cops in some of their home countries aren't as friendly as we are. I think you should split up. You'll cover more ground that way. Is that OK, Agnes?" Maguire said.

"Yes, of course. The pubs and restaurants will be opening up now, so we best get going before they get too busy with the lunchtime trade," Gallagher said.

"Right. Off you go then, and if you get anything significant, call me. OK?"

"Yes, boss," they said in unison.

Maguire went back to her desk and answered a few emails that had come in from the Garda Headquarters in Dublin. She didn't notice the time slipping by, but her desk phone rang again just before noon. She answered it with the customary salutation.

"Hi, Deirdre. It's me again. I've been doing some poking around on the car," McNally said.

"Oh, nice. That was quick. Anything?"

"Yes. Quite a bit. It is, or was, a Toyota Avensis. The model year is 2001, and it's a black two litre diesel. But you knew all that anyway. But here's something else. It more or less dropped off the radar about nine months ago. It hasn't been taxed, insured, or NCT'd since. It was traded in with a dealer called Kenny's Karz – spelt K-A-R-Z. It's out near Cloona, just off the N59. The place is run by Jim Kenny. I've looked him up on DoneDeal. He seems to specialize in end-of-life stock. He has four bangers on offer just now. To be honest, it just looks like he's trading from the side of his house. A real 'kerbside motors' operation."

"Wow! That's fantastic, Eoin. I'm not even going to ask how you got all that information, but thanks a bunch. That's very useful. Will I see you later?" Maguire said.

"Yes, that would be nice. I'll call you nearer going home time."

"Great. Chat then."

Maguire wasted no time in bringing the new information to her boss.

"Cripes, he's keen, Deirdre. Looks like a keeper to me," O'Shea said.

"Well, never mind all that. Do you want to come with me? I'm going out to see Mr Kenny and his crazy cars operation, or whatever."

"Yes, I'll come too."

* * *

It was a warm, overcast day as O'Shea and Maguire drove north on the N59. Grey clouds promising rain hung high over the land, making the atmosphere muggy and close.

"Where exactly is this place, anyway?" O'Shea said.

"We turn off to the right a bit further on. It's called the Ballinrobe Road. It's very narrow, but it eventually leads back into Castlebar after a good bit of wandering about. Cloona is just a few kilometres after the turn," Maguire said, consulting Google Maps on her phone.

They found the Ballinrobe road and turned right off the N59.

"Cripes, I see what you mean," O'Shea said, "are you sure this is right?"

"Yep! Just keep going; Kenny's place isn't too far now."

O'Shea steered the car along the single-track road. It was obviously little used, as grass had grown up in the middle of it, and it was pockmarked, with some deep potholes where heavy rain had broken up the already uneven surface. As they rounded a sharp right-hand bend, they spotted a small collection of ancient vehicles resting in the grass on the left-hand side, adjacent to a modest bungalow. When they pulled up, they could see hand-written notices in the windscreens of the cars with prices and very brief observations, such as "Economical"; "Just three owners", and "Taxed" scrawled in black marker pen.

"This must be it," Maguire said.

They both got out of O'Shea's car and walked to the front door of the rather weather-beaten bungalow. O'Shea knocked firmly on the half-glazed entrance.

After a couple of minutes, a shadow appeared in the glass, and the door was opened by a man who looked to be in his fifties. He was overweight and poorly dressed in a greasy blue shirt that was not tucked into his well-worn denim jeans. He had badly scuffed work boots on his feet, and it looked as if he hadn't shaved in several days, with grey stubble adorning his round, ruddy face.

O'Shea held up his warrant card.

"My name is DI Martin O'Shea, and this is my colleague DS Maguire from Westport. We're looking for a Jim Kenny."

The man looked rather suspiciously at the two detectives and then said somewhat reluctantly, "Well, you've found him. I'm Jim Kenny. What can I do for you?" he said, without making any attempt to invite them in.

"We are making enquiries about a black Toyota Avensis that you may have sold recently, Mr. Kenny. Do you remember it at all?" O'Shea said.

"Do you have the registration number?"

"No, but we have the VIN number if that helps."

"Ah, it doesn't matter. I remember the car anyway. You don't get many of them in black," Kenny said.

"Tell me about the car then, Mr Kenny."

"Call me Jim, Inspector. Everyone does."

"OK, Jim, so what about the car?"

"Bloody thing cost me, didn't it? I took it as a trade-in on a nice, clean Mercedes Sprinter van I had here. I gave the lad €800 for it. But it was a wreck. The thing was smoking like a trouper, and it was overheating and everything. It was lying there for ages, and then this punter comes along about two weeks ago and says he wants to buy it. Gave me €400 for it, that's all, but he didn't seem to care about the condition or anything. Said he just wanted cheap transport for a few days."

"I see. Do you have this man's name – the buyer, I mean?" O'Shea said.

"Eh, no. But I don't think he was a local man. I had never seen him before, and he didn't have a Mayo accent," Kenny said.

"What about the paperwork then? He must have filled out the change of ownership document."

"Ah, to be honest, he didn't want to bother with any of that. Just gave me the cash and drove it out. Mind you, I had to jump start it for him, but he went eventually, and I was glad to see the back of him and the car."

Maguire, who had been listening to the exchange between her boss and the car dealer, decided to speak up.

"Can you describe the buyer, Mr Kenny?" she said.

"Ah, he was just average. Brown hair. Not quite as tall as your man here, but I wasn't looking too closely at him. I was just glad to be getting rid of that old heap, to be honest."

"Is there nothing else you can tell us about him? How did he get here, for example? You're not exactly on a main road," Maguire persisted.

"I dunno. Funny thing that. He just sort of turned up."

O'Shea decided that there was little more to be gained from talking to Jim Kenny, so he brought matters to a close.

"You need to be a bit more careful about keeping records, Jim. That vehicle was involved in a serious crime, and now, thanks to you, we have no idea who may have been responsible."

Before Kenny could respond, the two detectives turned and left him to his thoughts.

Chapter Nine

Agnes Gallagher and Liam Staunton divided the town of Westport in two. Staunton turned left out of the station, crossed the Carrowbeg river, and walked up along North Mall towards the large one-way system on the N59 that encircled the very centre of the town. Gallagher turned right out of the station and set off along Altamont Street, down High Street, and back up through John's Row that would take her back to where her colleague was working on the same grand circle formed by the N59.

When Gallagher called to her third premises, she thought she might be in luck. A Crúiscín Beag, which translated from Irish means the little jug, was a small café on the corner of High Street. It was a glass-fronted place, with three tables arranged outside on the footpath and several more inside on the bare stone floor. Round glass globes hung over the interior tables, with light bulbs that showed off bright orange wire filaments. It was painted a fashionable mid-grey colour, and was obviously popular as several tables were occupied with folks having various types of coffee and pastries. The counter was positioned along the back wall where the big and complicated-looking coffee machine hissed and gurgled as Americanos, Cappuccinos, Lattes, and other libations were prepared and dispensed. Behind the counter, two young women in their twenties, one fair and one dark, were very busy attending to their orders, and Gallagher had to wait quite some time before the fair-haired woman turned and asked her what she would like. It was clear from her accent that she was not a native of the town.

Gallagher held up her warrant card.

"My name is Detective Agnes Gallagher," she said, "may I ask your name?"

The woman seemed a little unsettled. She looked around to see who might have been listening before replying.

"My name in Klaudia Nowak. Am I in trouble?"

"No, not at all, Klaudia. I'm just wondering if you can help me, that's all."

"It's very busy right now, Sergeant. Could you come back? Or maybe I could come to you?" Nowak said.

Not to be put off so easily, Gallagher took one of the photographs of the red shoes that she had acquired from forensics and showed it to the woman.

"Yes, OK, I understand," Gallagher said, "but I'm just trying to locate the person who owned these shoes. They are quite distinctive. Do you think you might know who they belonged to?"

Nowak looked briefly at the photograph.

"Not now, please. Come back at three o'clock. Then we can talk."

With that, she turned her attention back to the hissing coffee machine and continued to prepare hot drinks for the customers.

Gallagher wasn't quite sure how to react. She could, of course, insist that Klaudia Nowak address the matter right now, but she felt that such a course of action would be counter-productive. The woman could just clam up, and then they would be none the wiser. She decided to do what Nowak had suggested, but she wasn't entirely happy about it.

Gallagher left the café and continued on up towards the N59. She called at two more venues but drew a complete blank. Feeling a little unsettled herself, she walked on up to the centre of the town where she bumped into her colleague.

"Hi, Liam. Any luck?"

"No, nothing. You?" Staunton said.

"I'm not sure." Gallagher went on to outline what had happened at An Crúiscín Beag.

Staunton said, "Hmm. OK, well, why don't both of us pay her a visit at three? It sounds as if she might know something."

"Good idea. Let's get some lunch in the meantime."

* * *

It was quiet in the Garda detectives' office, and Deirdre Maguire had, for once, time to think. She sat at her PC and thought. Then, she had an idea. She did some research on the worldwide web and found the address and phone number of the people who ran the Irish advertising site, Done Deal. She called the number, and after a few false starts when she was put through to the wrong people, she finally got to speak to an Edel Jordan, who described herself as the webmaster for the site. Maguire introduced herself.

"Edel, I wonder if you can help me. My name is Detective Sergeant Deirdre Maguire from the detective unit here in Westport, County Mayo. I'm enquiring about a specific listing you had on your site for a black Toyota Avensis being sold by an outfit called Kenny's Karz with a 'K' a few weeks ago."

"OK, Sergeant, and how can we help?" Jordan said.

"I don't suppose there's any chance that you could help me to identify the person who bought it?" But even as Maguire uttered the question, her heart was sinking.

"Well, I won't be able to say who bought the car, but I might be able to dig up some information on who looked at it and see if there were any messages sent to the seller from the platform. Would that help?"

"Oh, yes, it would. How long will that take, Edel?"

"If you hold on, I'll do it right now. Let me just see if I can locate the listing first. A black Avensis from Kenny's Karz, you say?"

"Yes, that's right."

"OK. Hold on, and let me look for you."

Maguire held on a little nervously. She really did think this was a long shot. A few minutes later, Edel Jordan came back to her.

"Right, well, I have the listing here. It was on for €800, and it's a black Avensis with a two-litre diesel engine, right?"

"Yes, that's it. What can you tell me from the listing?"

"It was viewed 62 times, which is very few for cars sold

on Done Deal. And I can see that one of the viewers sent a message to Kenny's offering €400, cheeky bugger! Then there's another message from Kenny telling the buyer to come and see the car, and they could talk about the price, and the buyer acknowledges that one."

"Is there any way of identifying the buyer, Edel?"

"Not by name, but I might be able to find the I.P. address the message was sent from if you give me a few minutes. Do you want to hold on, or will I call you back?"

"I'll hold if that's OK?"

"Right. I'll be as quick as I can."

"No hurry, Edel, and thanks," Maguire said.

Maguire was put on hold, and the inevitable lift music played annoyingly down the phone for what seemed like an age. Then Jordan was back on the line.

"Hello, Sergeant. Sorry for the delay. The I.P. address of the person who was interested in the car is 108.128.122.458 if that's any help?"

"That's great, Edel. How do I find out where that I.P. came from?

"I'm sorry I can't do that from here, but if you use 'Who is' or 'IP Lookup' on the net, you should be able to locate it. It's definitely Irish in any case."

That's terrific, Edel. Thank you so much; that's been very helpful."

"No problem, Sergeant. Anytime."

Maguire wasted no time in bringing up one of the search sites that Jordan had given her on her PC. She put in the IP address and waited for a few seconds while the software did its thing. Then, the screen filled with a display of lots of information about the location and nature of the numbers she had entered. Maguire studied it carefully and sent the page to the printer.

She collected the sheet of information and went to look for DI O'Shea, but he wasn't in his office.

Chapter Ten

Agnes Gallagher and Liam Staunton made their way back to An Crúiscín Beag a few minutes after three o'clock. The place was much quieter than it had been earlier, with just one table occupied by a middle-aged couple chatting over two cups of tea and some rather tasty-looking fruit scones.

Klaudia Nowak was behind the counter tidying up after a busy lunchtime service. She was stacking white coffee cups on top of each other over the coffee machine and wiping the surfaces down with a cloth and a bottle of spray cleaner. Gallagher approached the counter and spoke to the woman.

"Hello again, Klaudia. Is this a good time?"

Nowak turned around and put down her cleaning stuff.

"Oh, hello again. Yes, this is better. Can I get you and your colleague a coffee?"

"No, thanks, Klaudia. If we could just have a chat about the photo we showed you earlier."

"Yes, of course. Come over here."

The three of them went to a secluded table on the other

side of the café from the couple who were still chatting away merrily. Staunton asked Nowak, "So, Klaudia, the photo. What can you tell us?"

Nowak looked around a little nervously to make sure that no one was eavesdropping.

"The shoes. There is one girl that I have seen wearing those. She came in here a few times, and we talked. She is also from my country. What has happened to her?" Nowak said.

"What country is that, Klaudia?" Staunton said.

"I am originally from Poland, but my family moved across the border to Ostrava in Czechia when I was small. Maria is from Prague."

"Maria – that's the girl with the shoes, right?" Maguire said.

"Yes."

"When did you see her last, Klaudia?" Staunton asked.

"Not for at least a week, maybe more. Every day is the same here when it's busy. Time goes quickly."

"Do you know what Maria worked at or where she lived?" Maguire asked.

"I don't know exactly where she lived, but nearby, I think," Nowak said.

"And do you know what she worked at?" Maguire went on.

"I don't know if I should say. She might get into trouble."

"Don't worry about that. It's important that we find out, Klaudia," Maguire said.

Nowak looked around again and shifted restlessly in her seat. She was clearly a little uneasy with the conversation, but she didn't want to appear to be difficult with the local police.

"I think she was working as an escort girl," Nowak said.

"I see. Why do you think that, Klaudia?"

"She always had money and good clothes. And she hinted that she could introduce me to someone who could get me the same kind of work. She said it paid much better than here, but I'm not interested. I come from a good family, and that kind of thing doesn't interest me. Anyway, I have a boyfriend here. He is a farmer and a good man," the woman said, smiling.

"Did you ever discover her surname, Klaudia?" Maguire said.

"No, just Maria and that might not have been her real name at all."

"Hmm .. OK. Is there anything more you can tell us about this woman, Klaudia?" Staunton said.

"No. That's it. Sorry, I don't know more."

"Never mind. You have been very helpful. Thanks. If you think of anything more, or if anyone comes in looking for Maria, please let me know," Maguire said, handing over a business card.

"Yes, OK."

* * *

When they returned to the station, Gallagher and Staunton were keen to impart the information they had gleaned from the girl in the café. They both approached Maguire, who was back at her desk working the PC, to get as much information as she could about the location where the enquiries for the black Avensis had come from.

Gallagher said to Maguire, "Sarge, have you got a minute?"

"Sure, Agnes. What's up?"

Gallagher filled her boss in on the information about the wearer of the red shoes. Maguire raised an eyebrow in surprise.

"Wow! So, this girl could have been some kind of prostitute, then?"

"It looks a bit like that, boss," Gallagher replied.

"OK. I didn't know we had that sort of thing going on around here. Tell you what. Why don't you dig into it and see if you can find out if there's an escort service operating here in Westport? Start with advertising websites like Locanto or Vivastreet, and if you don't get any joy there, widen out the search a bit. What did you say the girl called herself?" Maguire said.

"Maria, but that could be a made-up name. But we do know that she's probably from Prague. Would the immigration people have anything on her, do you think, boss?"

"Worth a call, for sure. Can you both stay on it to see what emerges?"

Staunton and Gallagher replied in unison, "Yes, boss."

* * *

O'Shea eventually reappeared, and Maguire followed him into his office.

"Got a sec, boss?" she said.

"Yes, of course. Come in. Grab a seat. What's up?"

"I've got a location that was used by the bloke that bought the Avensis from Kenny's Karz. DoneDeal were helpful, and they gave me the IP address of where the enquiries came from. It's an internet café here in the town. A place called 'Fonenet' spelled with an F, and it's down by the river near the electric bike rental place."

"Good work, Deirdre. I think we should pay them a visit, don't you?"

"Yes. Definitely. Do you want to go now?"

"Give me a few minutes, then I'll be ready."

"OK. Give me a shout."

Five minutes later, O'Shea came out of his office and said to Maguire, "OK, Deirdre. Let's go. We'll take a squad car. It will look more official."

They drove up to the N59 and turned off down by The Old Mill hostel towards the river. They stopped the car at the roundabout where the bike rental shop was located. Fonenet was a very small shop with all sorts of electronic gadgets displayed in the brightly lit window. Inside, in the middle of the floor, there were four PCs arranged in a cross shape with high partitions between them to afford some minimal privacy to the users. Overhead though, Maguire spotted a dark glass globe with a red LED blinking on and off.

They approached the counter where a swarthy man with a dark beard, dark hair and eyes was poring over an iPhone that was undergoing surgery. O'Shea introduced himself, holding up his warrant card.

"Hi. My name is Detective Inspector Martin O'Shea, and this is my colleague, Detective Sergeant Maguire. Can you confirm that this premises uses the I.P. address, 108.128.122.458?"

"Yes. That's our main router for the internet PCs. Why do you ask?"

"Oh no, don't worry, you have done nothing wrong. But may I ask if your CCTV system is always on when the internet PCs are in use?" O'Shea said.

"Yes, of course. Why?" the man said.

"How long do you keep the recordings for?" O'Shea said.

"Long time. The camera has eight terabytes of storage, so it keeps enough for about six weeks. Then, it overwrites the oldest. I put the system in myself," he said with some obvious pride.

"Great. I wonder if you could give us a copy of the recordings from the last four weeks?"

"OK. Give me a few minutes. I'll copy it onto a USB thumb drive for you."

"Thanks," O'Shea said. He turned to Maguire.

"How long ago did Kenny say he sold the car, Deirdre?"

"I think it was about two weeks. He wasn't precise, but I'm fairly sure that's what he said."

"Great. So, we should have yer man on this lot then when we get it. Can you arrange for Agnes to trawl the video for around that time?" O'Shea said.

"Yes, but how will she know what to look for?" Maguire said.

"That depends on how good the video is. If we can see what sites the punter was looking at from the CCTV, then we should be able to narrow it down. And you could get back on to DoneDeal. They might be able to pinpoint the dates when that advert was last looked up."

"Good idea."

The shop manager returned with a small black SanDisk thumb drive and held it out for O'Shea.

"There you go. It's all on there, Inspector."

"Thanks. Do we owe you anything for the memory stick?" O'Shea said.

"No, no charge. We are always glad to help the police."

"Great thanks. May I ask your name?"

"Yes, of course. I'm Muhamad Hassan. I'm here most days except Friday."

"Thanks, Muhammad. Very helpful."

Chapter Eleven

Back at the Garda station, Agnes Gallagher and Liam Staunton were deep in conversation about how best to approach the seedier side of the sex trade in their local town.

"Let's look up those sites that the sarge suggested and see what we can find. But after that, Liam, it's over to you," Gallagher said.

"How do you mean?"

"Well, if we can find any local girls offering their services, there's no point in me trying to get an appointment with them, is there? That's down to you!" Gallagher said.

"Oh, I see what you mean. OK. Let's get started."

They took a site each, and were surprised to find that there appeared to be quite a few girls offering various services in the town, but non explicitly talking about sexual activity. But 'happy ending massages' seemed to feature quite a bit, as did 'full girlfriend experience'.

After forty-five minutes, they stopped their research to compare notes.

"What have you got, Liam?" Gallagher said.

"I have only five that look as if they could be of interest, and three of those claim to be visiting just for a short time. None of them is called Maria, though. What about you?"

"I got seven possibles. Let's see if any of them are the same."

The two detectives compared notes, and established that two of the advertisements seem to reference the same person, so they were left with just a handful of prospects.

"OK, so what now, Agnes?"

"I think you'd better start phoning them, Liam, and see if you can make appointments. You might even enjoy yourself!"

"Stop, will ya! This is weird enough already. OK. Leave me in peace then, and I'll see what I can do. I don't want you eavesdropping as I discuss my sexual preferences with a hooker!"

Gallagher just smiled at her colleague and left to get a cup of coffee.

Liam Staunton made the calls. He only managed to connect with two of the girls, but he made arrangements to visit them the following afternoon. They were both located centrally in the town, so he spaced them just an hour apart. He wasn't actually going to do anything with either of them - just chat, and see what he could find out about Maria, if that was her name.

* * *

When O'Shea and Maguire got back to the station, Maguire said, "I think I'd better look at the video. Agnes and Liam are busy," referring to the examination of the CCTV footage they had retrieved from Fonenet.

"In my office. But first, can you get back to DoneDeal? See if they can give us an approximate time and day when the ad for the Avensis was last looked up. That will make searching this lot a whole lot quicker," he said, holding up the memory stick.

"OK. I'll see what they can give us, and then I'll come and find you."

When O'Shea got back to his desk, there was a note telling him that a Mrs McGroarty from the town had been looking for him. A mobile number was scribbled on the piece of paper bearing her name. He lifted his phone and dialled.

After what seemed like quite a long time, the phone was answered by a woman with a strong country accent.

"Marjorie McGroarty here. Who's calling, please?"

"Ah, Mrs McGroarty, this is Detective Inspector Martin O'Shea from Westport. I believe you were looking for me."

"Oh, hello, Inspector. Yes, I was. Have you a minute?" the woman said.

"Yes, of course. How can I help?"

"Well, it's very odd, you see. I mean, I've had some funny ones before, but nothing like this. I don't know what to do."

"Sorry, Mrs McGroarty, what is very odd?" O'Shea said.

"It's the apartment. I can't get in touch with the woman who rented it, and she should be gone by now, but all her stuff is still there. And the bathroom is a mess."

"I see. So, you have an apartment that you rent out, is that right, Mrs McGroarty?"

"Yes, of course. Didn't I say? It's on Airbnb. The only reason I could give it to her was that I had a cancellation. So, I agreed to let her stay for two weeks. I wanted to see her give her back her deposit at the end of the time, but I couldn't reach her, and when I went round, the place still had her stuff in it, but no sign of yer one."

"Where is this apartment, Mrs McGroarty?" O'Shea said.

"It's on Tober Hill. All nice and newly refurbished. There are two flats in the one house, and she was supposed to be in the top one."

"I see. What number on Tober Hill would that be, Mrs McGroarty?"

"It's 22, of course. I have had it for about three years now, and it's very popular. Both apartments are let out for the whole summer."

"Mrs McGroarty, would you be able to meet me there in, say, twenty minutes? It could be important."

"Well, I suppose so, Inspector. What's the story?"

"I'll explain when we meet. And if I could ask you not to go inside for the moment until we get there," O'Shea said.

"Very well. If you think that's absolutely necessary. But I have been in already, you know," Mrs McGroarty said.

"Yes, that's fine, but it's best not to go back in for now. See you soon."

"Righto. See you then."

When O'Shea had finished the call, he went in search of Deirdre Maguire. She was at her desk nursing a mug of coffee.

"C'mon Deirdre, we need to go out. I'll explain along the way."

Chapter Twelve

When they arrived outside 22 Tober Hill, it was indeed exactly as Mrs McGroarty had described. It had obviously had a total refurbishment in the last few years, and now sported a dark grey hall door and matching modern window frames. The roof looked new too, but there was no sign of a chimney, indicating that the fireplaces, which would have been part of the original house had been removed.

They got out of the car and went across the road to the property. O'Shea knocked firmly on the front door, and a moment later, it was answered by a woman in her late fifties with short grey hair fashioned in a well-cut wave. The woman was stocky, if not obese, and was clad in a grey skirt and jacket with a pale yellow blouse beneath. She wore a string of pearls about her neck.

Maguire thought to herself, "A grey woman in a grey suit in a grey house. What's with all this grey?"

"Mrs McGroarty?" O'Shea said.

"Yes, and you must be Inspector O'Shea. Come in, won't you," the woman said totally ignoring Maguire.

"This is my colleague, Detective Sergeant Maguire," O'Shea said, gesturing to Maguire, but still McGroarty did not acknowledge her presence, other than with a rather snooty glance.

"Which apartment was the one you spoke to me about, Mrs McGroarty?" O'Shea said.

"It's upstairs. Follow me."

The three of them climbed the narrow stairway which was covered in the inevitable grey carpet. When they arrived on the first-floor landing, the door to the upper apartment was open. McGroarty stood aside and gestured for O'Shea to go in.

Once inside, O'Shea and Maguire could see what the owner had said. There were clothes scattered here and there around on the furniture. In the little kitchenette, evidence of ready meals that had been presumably microwaved was on the draining board, and there was a dirty plate in the sink along with some cutlery.

Maguire made her way into the bedroom, where she was greeted by a double bed covered in just a pale blue and white striped bedsheet. A duvet in a matching cover lay crumpled on the floor. On a small dressing table built into the wall beside the single wardrobe, some cosmetics were spread out, and Maguire noticed a few unopened packets of condoms, too.

The bathroom off the bedroom was in a bad state. There was about thirty centimetres of cold soapy water in the bath itself, and quite an amount of spillage on the floor that had been partly soaked up by a large grey bath towel that was pushed up against the bath. In the wash hand basin, there was what looked like blood stuck to the sides of the ceramics, and the mirror above the sink was cracked.

Maguire rejoined McGroarty and O'Shea, who were still in the living room.

"Boss. I think we need to seal this place up and get forensics out. There are signs of something unpleasant in the bathroom with what looks like blood in the basin," Maguire said.

Mrs McGroarty looked shocked and had gone a sort of grey colour herself.

"You can't do that. I have this place let out from tomorrow. What will I tell the arrivals?" she said in a high-pitched tone.

O'Shea was first to respond.

"I'm sorry Mrs McGroarty, but we have no choice. This may be a crime scene, and we need to have it examined thoroughly. Now, I'd like you to come down to the Garda station with me so that we can get a statement from you and find out a bit more about your most recent tenant. Sergeant Maguire will wait here until our forensic people arrive."

Maguire smiled inwardly. She didn't appreciate Mrs McGroarty's attitude, but she knew her boss would find a way of dealing with the woman that would put manners on her.

McGroarty and the inspector duly departed, with a little more grumbling coming from the owner, leaving Maguire alone on the upstairs landing. She called her colleagues in the forensic lab in Castlebar and asked them to come out as soon as they could to do a thorough sweep of the apartment. She got through to Kevin Walsh almost immediately.

"Hi, Kevin. I'm here at number 22 Tober Hill in Westport. We're investigating a potential murder case, and I need your team out here to do an examination of an apartment. Is there anyone available?" Maguire said.

"Hi, Deirdre. Yes, that's no problem. I can come out myself and bring Sinéad with me. If we need more bodies, I can call them from there. What have you got so far?" Walsh said.

"I'm not sure, Kevin. It looks as if there may have been some kind of fracas here in the flat, and there may possibly be a connection to a case we are investigating, but it's early days. How long will you be?"

"We should be there in about 45 minutes. See you then."

"Great. Thanks."

When she had finished the call, Maguire donned vinyl gloves and overshoes and went back into the apartment. She made for the bedroom, and carefully searched the dressing table drawer, the chest of drawers that was placed against the wall, and the small white wardrobe that looked as if it had arrived from IKEA recently. She found little of interest. There was a small amount of clean underwear in the top drawer of the chest, and just two summer outfits hanging in the wardrobe, along with a pair of shoes and another pair of trainers. Both were size 5, and looked fairly new. Feeling a little despondent, but keen to fill the time waiting for the forensic team to do something useful, she positioned herself at the side of the bed, bent her knees, and heaved the mattress up in the air, craning her neck to see if there was anything underneath. She spotted a small zipped bag lying on the bed's base. It was a dark brown colour, and Maguire reckoned it could be a make-up bag or maybe a small wash bag.

Struggling with the weight of the mattress, Maguire managed to move it so that it was askew on the bed, and she was able to reach underneath it and retrieve the little bag. When she opened it, she was surprised to find that it contained €780 in mixed €20 and €50 notes. She took a plastic evidence bag out of her pocket, and dropped it into it. When Kevin and Sinéad arrived, she would get one of them to dust it for fingerprints.

While she continued to fill the time, she went back downstairs and knocked on the door of the lower apartment. There was no reply, so she put her ear to the door and could hear no sound coming from inside. She knocked again with the same result, so she took a calling card out of her pocket, wrote 'Please call me asap' on it, and pushed it under the door.

By that time, Kevin Walsh and his colleague had arrived outside, so Maguire directed them upstairs. Kevin Walsh was a tall man in his early thirties, slim and fit-looking with a shock of fair curly hair. He always seemed to be in good humour despite some of the gruesome scenes he was often faced with, and his colleague, Sinéad, who was about the same age but with shoulder length blonde hair seemed to reflect his buoyant good form.

"We need to give this place a thorough going over, Kevin. I've had a quick look around, and I'm not sure, but I think there may be some blood residue in the basin of the bathroom," Maguire said.

"OK, no problem. We'll see what we can find. Are you staying?" Walsh said.

"No, I need to get back to the station but call me if you find anything of interest. I'll leave you to it."

Maguire bid farewell to Walsh and Sinéad Brennan.

Chapter Thirteen

Back at the Garda station, O'Shea had shown Mrs McGroarty to an interview room and offered her refreshments. She grumbled a bit at the formality of the situation, saying, "This is all a bit over the top, Inspector. After all, I have done nothing wrong."

"I won't keep you any longer than necessary, Mrs McGroarty, and of course, you are free to leave at any time, but it would be very helpful if we could get some details of the person who rented your Airbnb, and has now apparently, disappeared," O'Shea said.

"Very well. Let's get on with it then," the woman said, failing to hide her frustration.

The two of them took seats at opposite sides of the green-topped table as Mrs McGroarty sipped her coffee.

O'Shea began his questioning.

"So, what can you tell me about this woman, Mrs McGroarty? For example, did she give you her full name and an address?"

"She called herself Maria Jones, but I doubt if that was

her real name. She spoke with a distinct foreign accent, though don't ask me where she was from. I'm not good with that kind of thing."

"How did she make the booking?" O'Shea went on.

"She found my place on the web, and then she phoned me. As I said, the apartment is usually booked up all summer, but I had a cancellation, so I agreed to let her have it for two weeks."

"So, you would have her phone number on your mobile phone then?" O'Shea asked.

"Eh, yes, I suppose so."

"How did she pay you?"

"In cash, when she arrived. I always prefer cash wherever possible. You never know with these types, do you?"

"What did the woman look like, Mrs McGroarty?"

"She was pretty. Blonde curly hair, though, of course, that was probably dyed. A good figure as far as I could judge, and although she was clearly foreign, her English was very good with just a hint of an accent. She did ask me an odd question, though," Mrs McGroarty said.

"And what was that?"

"She asked me if there was any CCTV monitoring the house."

"And is there?" O'Shea said.

"No, of course not. Why would I need to have that sort of thing? My guests are just holidaymakers here for a couple of days enjoying the scenery and the restaurants."

"Did Ms Jones say what the purpose of her visit to Westport was?"

"Heavens above, Inspector, I don't interrogate my

tenants like that. I just rent out the place. What they get up to when they are staying there is their own affair."

"Do you know if Ms Jones had a car?"

"I don't think so. She was walking and towing a small black wheelie thing when she arrived. I imagined that she had arrived by train or bus."

"Is there anything else you can tell me about this woman, Mrs McGroarty?" O'Shea said.

"No. That's all I know. But more importantly, when am I going to get the place back? I have bookings to honour, you know."

"I think it's probably best if you cancel your booking for a few days, Mrs McGroarty. Our forensic team are out there now examining the place, but they may need to come back, depending on what they find."

"But that's ridiculous! You can't just take over my house like that. I have a good mind to put in a complaint!" she said, her face getting red with indignation.

"That's up to you, Mrs McGroarty. I assure you we won't be there any longer than necessary. We're pretty busy too, you know. But there is a possibility that a crime may have been committed at your property, so until we know more, it has to remain at our disposal. Before you go, could I ask you to look up your mobile phone and give me Ms Jones' number please?"

She fished the phone out of her handbag, put on spectacles, and scrolled down through her recent call history on the phone.

"I think this is it. 0847889121, but I've tried ringing it. It just keeps going to voicemail, and then it says the mailbox is full."

O'Shea wrote the number into his notebook.

"Thank you. We'll look into it," he said.

McGroarty shrugged and muttered something under her breath.

* * *

O'Shea saw Mrs McGroarty off the premises and arranged a lift for her back to Tober Hill. Despite her protestations, he felt that the woman was enjoying the drama that she had unwittingly become involved in. No doubt, tongues would be wagging around the town later on.

Back in the office, O'Shea approached Maguire who had returned whilst he was interviewing the landlady.

"Hi, Deirdre. What's the story out beyond?"

"Hi, boss. Kevin and Sinéad are out there now exploring. I found a wee make-up bag under the mattress with €780 in it. I gave it to Kevin to examine for prints. He's going to call me later. What have you been up to?"

O'Shea filled Maguire in on his discussion with Mrs McGroarty.

"This Airbnb thing is nuts, Deirdre. There's no proper registration process for it or anything. You could be letting God knows what into your property," O'Shea said.

"I know. It's no help to us, that's for sure. But the landlords don't care. They make barrow loads of money from it, and they don't ask too many questions. Wasn't there one recently that was turned into a grow house?"

"Yes, I read about that. Anyway, what are you up to?"

"I'm just about to start with the CCTV from Fonenet. Care to join me?" Maguire said.

"No, you're OK, thanks. I'd better go upstairs and put the Super in the picture. He'll be anxious for us to make some real progress with this. I think the tourism people are bending his ear over it. It's not great publicity for the area. Listen, can you arrange a briefing for, say, four o'clock? We need to coordinate with everyone and share whatever we know by then."

"Yes, no problem. I'll tell Liam and Agnes. Do you want Kevin to come across too?" Maguire said.

"See what he says. It could be handy, but if he's very busy, it doesn't matter. Just get whatever he has to report from Tober Hill. Have they got anything more from Bartra where the body was found?" O'Shea said.

"I'll check with him when I'm talking to him."

"Thanks. See you later then."

Chapter Fourteen

As arranged, O'Shea brought the four of them together in the open plan at just after 4 pm.

"Right, everyone. Let's see what we have. Can we start with you, Liam?" O'Shea said.

"Yes, boss, of course. I have made appointments with two of the local girls from the website for tomorrow afternoon to see if I can find out anything about the deceased. Are we sure she was operating as an escort, sir?"

"Not one hundred percent, but it looks like that. Have we got anything from Kevin Walsh from the apartment, Deirdre."

"Yes, boss. He called me about half an hour ago. It is blood in the sink. He's having it analysed at the moment, and he is going to match it to what was left of the woman's body. But that won't be conclusive if it's just an ordinary blood group. He'll do better with the DNA, but that will take a couple of days. He also said that there are semen stains on the bed from at least three different people. So, what with the condoms we found, the semen stains, the money, and the dodgy name she used - chances are," Maguire said.

"OK. I got the deceased's mobile phone number from the landlady. Agnes, can you get onto the service provider and see if you can get a list of calls? I'm most interested in any incoming calls she received the day she was killed."

"Yes, boss. I'll get on it straight after this," Gallagher said.

"Deirdre, anything from the CCTV from the internet café?" O'Shea said.

"I'm still going through it, boss. Could you have a look at it with me when we are done here? There might be something, but it needs another pair of eyes."

"Sure, no problem. Mrs McGroarty identified the woman as Maria Jones. But I think we can discount the surname as being made up. Let's just call her Maria for now. And I was up with the Super, too. He's desperate for something positive to report, and I don't mean about prostitution in Westport. He wants to put out a statement. You know, the kind of thing, 'an isolated incident' or 'an unfortunate accident', whatever will keep the media happy. But we need to start with the perpetrator. We can't do much for the hapless Maria now, other than bring her killer to book. OK, everyone, let's get on it."

* * *

"What do you want me to look at, Deirdre?" O'Shea said as the meeting broke up.

"Over here, boss. On my PC."

The two of them walked across to Maguire's desk and

drew up a couple of chairs. Maguire fiddled with the machine until she had the CCTV frozen at a particular frame.

"Here. We can see chummy at the computer, and I can just about make out the DoneDeal banner at the top of the screen, but I can't see what exactly he's looking at. But he has a piece of paper on the desk beside him, and he's writing something down. Now, if I roll the tape forward slowly, see if you can tell what it is that he's making a note of," Maguire said.

O'Shea leant in closer to the screen and studied it closely.

"Stop it there, Deirdre. Wind it back a bit. That's it. Now, forward again, slowly."

Maguire did as she was told, and then O'Shea looked up.

"His handwriting isn't fabulous, but it looks like Kenny's Karz," O'Shea said.

"Yes, that's what I thought. That must be the bloke that bought the Avensis then," Maguire said.

"Yes, I guess so. Have we a shot of his face?"

"No such luck. He has that pesky baseball cap pulled well down. But I can see that he's not very tall, and he's a skinny little guy, too. What would you say, about 170cm or 5'7"?"

"Yeah, as far as we can tell. But it's not much of a description to go on. But it's better than nothing. And it tells us quite a bit more about him too," O'Shea said.

"Such as?"

"Well, he either hasn't got access to a computer of his own or if he has, he wants to make very sure his activity can't be traced on it. So, if I'm right, he's not a local resident. Most of the local low-life would know how to source a car without having to buy one from the lovely Mr Kenny."

"Good point. Do you think he's a blow in, then?" Maguire said.

"Could be. Print off a few stills from the CCTV. They aren't much to go on, but let's circulate them in any case. We might get lucky."

"Yes, OK. Then I'm going to call it a day if that's OK?" Maguire said.

"Oh, I see. Heavy date planned then?" O'Shea said, smiling.

"I couldn't possibly comment!"

* * *

Maguire's 'heavy date' was with her boyfriend, Eoin McNally. He mainly investigated bogus personal injury claims, but sometimes, he had to look into other questionable matters. It was during one of these that he had met Deirdre Maguire, and they had been out together a number of times and had got along very well.

This evening, they had decided to drive out as far as Murrisk to a much-publicised gastro-pub called The Tavern for dinner. McNally was going to collect Maguire at 7 pm, so she had time for a quick dash to the hairdressers before going home to finish preparations. By 6:50, she was fully ready for her date, dressed in a well-fitted cross-over yellow summer dress with a floral pattern set off with a solid gold locket that her father had given her for her twenty-first birthday, and a matching gold bangle. She did one final check in the mirror and liked what she saw.

McNally arrived at a few minutes past the hour and when she answered the door to him, he almost gasped.

"Wow! Hi Deirdre. You look amazing," and he leant in and gave her a gently kiss on the cheek, inhaling her subtle perfume as he did so.

"Hi, Eoin. Ready for off?"

"Yup. Let's go!"

McNally held the door of his car for her before settling into the driver's seat and taking off. It was a fine, bright evening as they drove out westwards past Knockahara and on towards Glenco. When the road joined to the coast, the deep blue of the Atlantic Ocean, reflecting the sky above, made a magnificent backdrop to the rugged coastline.

The Tavern Bar was located at the side of a long straight stretch of the R335, close to the access point for Croagh Patrick, the site of the rugged mountain beloved by pilgrims to this day. There has been a church on the top of the mountain since the 5th century, and it is said that Saint Patrick, the patron saint of Ireland, spent 40 days and nights on the mountain fasting.

McNally opened the car door again for Maguire, and the two of them stood for a moment admiring their surroundings. McNally took her hand, and said, "Gosh, Deirdre, it's a very beautiful place where we live. We are very lucky to be here."

Maguire squeezed his hand and moved closer to him, and they remained like that for several moments, just enjoying the peace of the place and the closeness.

Once they were seated in the restaurant and had ordered

their food, McNally asked, "So, what are you working on at the moment, Deirdre?"

"I'm still on that business out at Bartra with the burnt-out car."

"Oh, right. We have a claim in on that one, too."

"Really? Who's claiming what?" she said.

"It seems the car park where the fire happened is actually owned by the caravan site, even though the council maintain it. So, the owners of the site are claiming for damage to the car park. They say they'll have to have the whole area re-surfaced at a cost of around €10,000."

"But surely, the council will do that for nothing if it even needs it? When I was out there, it didn't seem that bad. There are some burn marks and blackening on the surface, but I'd say it will just wear away with the rain," Maguire said.

"My point exactly. But these things are never straightforward, as you know. Anyway, we are at least rejecting the claim for now."

"Who owns the caravan site?"

"A man by the name of Gerry McGroarty. He has a bit of history with us, so we are inclined to look into each of his claims quite carefully," McNally said.

"McGroarty! His wife doesn't happen to run an Airbnb in Westport by any chance, does she?"

"I couldn't say. But I could find out if it's important."

Just then, their food arrived, putting an end to their conversation for the moment. They both tucked in. The food was delicious.

Chapter Fifteen

Liam Staunton wasn't entirely happy about the task he had been set. He was quite a good-looking man, and had never had any trouble getting dates with women of his own age from around the town. He had no long-term relationship on the go at the moment, but he certainly didn't want word getting around that he had been visiting call girls.

The first appointment he had arranged was with a girl calling herself Avelina. She had told him to call her from the centre of Westport ten minutes before the scheduled meet, and she would give him final directions. When he made the call, he was directed to a shop on Mill Street close to the monument. There was a faded blue door beside the shopfront, and two bells set into a device in the door frame. His instructions were to ring the top bell in the small intercom unit and wait.

His ring was answered by a woman with a husky, sensuous voice.

"Is that you, Liam?" she said.

"Yes. Is that Avelina?"

"Come on up. The first door on the right at the top of the stairs."

The door buzzed, and Staunton pushed it open, finding himself in a narrow, dimly lit hallway with just one bare low-wattage bulb suspended from the ceiling to illuminate the space. The stairs was covered in faded red carpet that had seen better days, and the sides where there was exposed wood was dusty and chipped. Staunton was quite uncomfortable already, and he hadn't even got to the woman yet.

As he approached the door at the top of the stairs, it opened slowly. A tall woman with long dark hair and an amazing figure, dressed in Denim shorts and a bikini top pulled the door open further.

"Hi, Liam. Come in. I have been expecting you," she said, smiling warmly.

The room Staunton entered was in stark contrast to the entrance of the premises. It was bright and clean with new furniture, the biggest piece being a double bed in an alcove beside the chimney breast. An air freshener was doing its work very effectively, giving the atmosphere a fresh and pleasant feeling.

"So, Liam, what do you want to do today? Massage? Hand-job? BJ? or full service. That will be extra, of course," Avelina said, coming in close to him, so that he could smell her expensive perfume.

"I'm sorry, Avelina. I'm not here for any of those things. I just need to ask you for some information, but I'll pay you for your time, of course," Staunton said.

"What! Are you police or something?" she said, her voice

having risen an octave or two. She retreated back into her own space, looking shocked.

"That doesn't matter, and I'm not here to cause you any trouble. I just want information."

Avelina looked away, and sat down on one of the two chairs that were arranged in front of a small kitchen table. She crossed her legs and folded her arms across her chest.

"What do you want to know?" she said grumpily.

"There was a girl that died in a car fire out at Bertra beach a little while ago. We think her name was Maria, and she might have been from Poland or Czechia. We think she may have been working here in the same sort of thing you are doing. Did you know her?" Staunton said.

"No. I don't know her. Why do you think I would?" Avelina said rather indignantly.

"I don't know. I thought there might be some communication between the girls working as escorts here in the town. You know, talking amongst you about punters who were a bit dodgy. That sort of thing."

"No. Definitely not. And I can look after myself, thank you. I have my own system."

Staunton didn't want to know whatever that might be.

"So, how does all this work, Avelina?" Staunton said.

"How do you mean?"

"Well, how do you get your business?"

"It's simple. I rent a holiday flat for two weeks in towns around the country. Then I put my details and some photos up on the websites and wait for the phone to ring. It doesn't take long," Avelina said.

"So, are you just here for two weeks?"

"Yes. Then I move to another town. Use another name.

It's simpler that way. No trouble with the police. But now I will leave tomorrow because you have come to me."

"I'm sorry to disrupt your plans. But are you sure you don't know of this woman who died? She wore expensive red shoes."

Avelina laughed.

"Is that all you can tell me? Have you a photograph of her?"

"No, I'm sorry, I don't," Staunton said.

Avelina just shrugged.

"OK, then. I'd better be going," Staunton said. He stood up and reached into his trouser pocket pulling out a crisp €50 note and placing it on the table. Avelina looked at it and said, "Are you sure you wouldn't like to have some fun, Liam? I'm very good. I can relax you like nothing else."

"No thanks. It's fine. Is €50 enough?"

"Yes, thank you. Of course."

When Staunton left the woman, he couldn't help but daydream about her a little. She was very attractive, and he was sure that she could indeed have 'relaxed' him. But he cut off those thoughts quickly. Heaven knows what kind of trouble he could have brought down upon himself if he had given in to temptation. Anyway, his next appointment with a woman calling herself Hanna was coming up. He walked back down Mill Street and into a small coffee shop to gather his thoughts and get some refreshment.

Chapter Sixteen

O'Shea came out of his office and said to Maguire, "Deirdre, can we just go over a few things on this Bertra Beach business?"

"Yes, of course, boss. Your office?" Maguire said.

"Yes, please."

When they were both seated in O'Shea's office, Maguire was first to speak.

"What's on your mind, boss?"

"I'm not sure. But I feel a bit uneasy about this McGroarty thing. It's a bit of a coincidence, and you know I don't like those."

"Wait. Gerry McGroarty owns the caravan site, and his wife owns the apartment where we think this Maria woman was staying. Do either of them crop up in any other aspect of the enquiry, Deirdre?"

"Well, the only lead we have is the dude that bought the car from Kenny's Karz, and as far as I know, there's no connection between him and the McGroartys."

"Have we had anything back from forensics from the flat?"

"No, not yet. I'll follow up on it as soon as we are finished here. Is there anything else, boss?"

"I don't know, Deirdre. We don't seem to be getting anywhere with this thing, and the Super is going crazy. Any word back from Liam?"

"No. He's still out chatting up call girls, at least, I hope that's all he's doing!"

O'Shea smiled.

"Well, whatever he's up to, let's hope he gets some decent information for us. Bring me some good news, and soon, Deirdre, very soon."

"Yes, boss."

* * *

It was nearly time for Staunton's next appointment. High Street in Westport is a mixture of private houses and small shops that occupy the ground floor of the modest buildings. The street is steep, so the entrances and roof lines are stepped, but the houses properties are in excellent condition and are all brightly painted.

Staunton climbed the hill as far as number eighteen. The house had a bright blue door with paler blue paint on the rest of the outside of the building. All of the decor was in excellent condition. There were two bells mounted on the door frame, one above the other. Each bell had an illuminated label, and the topmost displayed the single letter 'H', which Staunton assumed was for Hanna. He pressed it once and stood back from the door. A moment later, there was a click, and he was able to push the door open when he found himself in front of a steep wooden staircase. He climbed up, and a door to his left opened when he reached the landing.

Staunton was expecting a woman similar to Alena, but he was in for a surprise. Standing in the doorway was the most beautiful woman he had ever set eyes on. She was around 5'4" tall, with almost white blonde hair to her shoulders, and the biggest, most striking pale blue eyes you could imagine. She had full, cupid-bow lips, and a round face with high cheekbones. Hanna was wearing a white sleeveless shirt-blouse, completely unbuttoned but still largely concealing her small breasts, and blue denim jeans that hugged her stunning figure in all the right places.

She reached out, took Liam Staunton's hand, and drew him into the room. The door clicked shut behind him. When they were both inside, Hanna closed in on Staunton, put her bare arms around his neck, and whispered in a very sexy voice, "What would you like to do today, Liam?"

Staunton was struggling. His natural desires were fighting with his Garda training, and for a minute, he wasn't sure which was winning. But a moment later, he put his hands on the girl's hips and moved her back half a metre.

"I'm sorry, Hanna. I just want to talk, if that's OK?"

"Of course. But I'm sorry, we must get the business out of the way first. How long do you want to talk for?"

"Can we start with half an hour and see how it goes?"

"Yes, no problem. That will be €80."

Staunton fumbled in his trouser pocket for the money. He took out a wad of €20 notes, and peeled off four of them. Hanna's eyes watched carefully.

"You can give me a tip later if you are happy with me," she said.

"Can we sit down, Hanna?"

The woman went to the table in the centre of the small room, sat on a kitchen styled chair, and gestured for Staunton to do the same.

"I'm sorry, Hanna, but would you mind buttoning your shirt?"

"What? You don't like me?" she said in an offended tone.

"No. Of course, I do. You are amazingly beautiful, but I don't want to be distracted while we talk. You see, I am a policeman," he said. He reached into another pocket and produced his warrant card.

Hanna's hands flew to her face, and she started to cry.

"Oh, God," she whimpered, "am I in trouble?"

"No. Not at all. As far as I can see, you have done nothing wrong. Nothing at all. But I need to ask you some questions about another woman who is working in the town, that's all."

"You are not going to arrest me?" she said, cheering up again quickly.

"No, of course not. I'm just here to get your help. Then I will leave you alone, and I promise you're not in trouble. Tell me a little about yourself, Hanna."

"I am from Czechia. I have a little boy who is six at home, and I live with my mother. My father is dead, and the father of Johann is gone, so the three of us just live in a town near the border."

"And how come you are here in Westport?" Staunton said.

"I come to Ireland every few months and work for two weeks. I can earn enough in that time to keep the three of us in food and clothes for three months or more. And I pay for Johann's school, too."

"But you are so beautiful. You could easily have a rich husband in Czechia; then you wouldn't have to do this."

"Yes, and get punched and beaten and locked up in some villa where I have no freedom. This is better. When I do the work, I think of my mother and Johann and the things I will be able to buy for them, and it's not too bad. And Irish men are usually kind to me. One time, a businessman in Limerick gave me €1000 as a tip, and they don't hit me like Johann's father did."

Staunton's heart was melting. He could only guess at the hardships this beautiful woman had been through in her young life. But he needed to get on with his mission.

"OK. So, I'm wondering if you know anything of another woman who was working here recently in Westport. Her name was Maria, we think, and she was staying in an apartment here in the town?"

"Have you a photograph of her?" Hanna said.

"No, I'm sorry. I'm afraid she was killed and then burnt with just her feet left, and a pair of good red shoes."

Hanna's hand went to her mouth.

"Oh my God. That's terrible. Poor girl."

"Yes. So, you see, Hanna, not everyone in this country is kind. Did you hear anything about this woman?"

Hanna looked down at the floor, so Staunton went on, "Please Hanna, we need to find out what happened to her, and who did this."

Hanna looked up after a few moments.

"There are a small number of girls from near where I live in Czechia that come to Ireland like me. We are not really friends, but we do talk to each other. It's so we can stay safe, and warn each other if there are bad clients around. We have a WhatsApp group."

"And did any of you hear anything about Maria?"

"We heard that a gang was trying to move in to control this business here in Ireland. They sent a couple of women to Ireland, and they were trying to take over our business and take our money," Hanna said.

"I see. And do you know anything more about this gang, Hanna?"

Hanna shuffled uneasily in her seat.

"I want to help you, Liam, but I'm afraid," she said.

"I understand. But just a name would help, and they won't find out where we got it from."

Hanna went to her bedside locker, opened a drawer, and took out a small black notebook. She thumbed through to a particular page, and handed it, open, to Staunton.

Staunton copied the name into his own notebook and gave it back to her.

"Thanks, Hanna. We will be very discreet. You can trust me."

Hanna smiled and said, "Now, you still have some credit, Liam. Would you like me to relax you?"

"I would love it, but I can't," he said, standing up to go.

Hanna moved in close to Staunton and kissed him softly on the lips.

"If you change your mind, I will be here for a few more days."

Staunton got up and made his way reluctantly to the

door. Just as he was about to leave, he turned to Hanna and said, "I don't suppose you'd be free for a drink later on?"

Hanna smiled.

"I'm not sure. But give me your number, and I'll call you if I am."

"Great. Just a drink and a chat now, nothing more."

Staunton scribbled his own personal mobile number on the back of a card and handed it to her. Hanna just stood in the doorway, smiling at him as he left the building.

Chapter Seventeen

"Hello, is that Sergeant Maguire?" the man's voice said.

"Yes, who's calling, please?"

"Hi, Sarge, it's Kevin here from forensics."

"Oh, sorry, Kevin, I didn't recognise your voice," Maguire said.

"No problem. We've been doing a bit more work on that burnt out car that was found down at Bertra beach. I have a few interesting things that we found. Are you free if I popped over for a few minutes?"

"Yes, sure, Kevin. Thanks. I'll see if DI O'Shea is free, too. See you soon."

"Yes, I'll be there in a few minutes."

When the call was over, Maguire went to find DI O'Shea. She located him in the small kitchen that was installed at the back of the open plan area, where they could make tea and coffee, and reheat stuff in a small microwave oven.

"Hi, boss. I've had a call from Kevin in forensics. He's

on his way over with some new information about the car from Bertra Beach. Are you free to sit in?" Maguire said.

"Yes, of course. I had words with the boss earlier. He's peppering. It's not him. I think he's getting heat from the locals about the incident. But you know how it is. It will all die down when something else comes along."

"OK. Well, here's Kevin now. Let's go into your office."

* * *

Kevin Walsh had a folder under his arm. When he was seated in O'Shea's office, he opened the folder.

"We've done a good bit of extra work on the car now. There are a few things to report. The most important thing is that we found a used sticking plaster on the floor, tucked down by the outside edge of the driver's seat. It's not very old, and there's a smear of blood on it, so we've sent it off to have a DNA profile prepared from it."

"Wow!" Maguire said. "Do you think it could be from the driver?"

"Yes, I do. It would be almost impossible for that to get there if it belonged to the passenger. And we can tell it was attached to someone just a few days ago, so it's not from the previous owner either. And there's more."

"Go on, Kevin. Don't keep us in suspense," Maguire said.

"Well, we managed to get some prints off the indicator stalk. It was on the outside of the steering wheel, and it escaped the fire. Fire is very peculiar. It always throws up enigmas for us. But there's something odd about this, too."

"What, Kevin?" Maguire said, feeling that he was milking it a bit.

"It looks as if he gripped the indicator stalk with his forefinger and thumb. That's unusual. Think about how you drive. If you're like me, you keep your hands on the wheel when you are using the indicators, and use your long fingertip to operate the stalk. But this guy appears to have gripped it with his finger and thumb."

"How do you know the prints are from the same person?" O'Shea asked.

"Ah. That's where it gets clever. Columbia University in the US has been doing work with AI, and has used it to identify prints from different fingers on the same hand. We sent the samples over to them. They were delighted to have a real case to work on. They came back last night and said that there was a ninety percent chance or better that it was the same person."

"Terrific. But what does that mean?" O'Shea said.

"I'd say the driver was quite inexperienced. Maybe a learner, or someone who isn't used to driving at all. Perhaps a young person."

"OK," O'Shea said, "that's useful, but doesn't really get us much further on. How long will the DNA thing take, Kevin?"

"We should have it back tomorrow. They put it to the top of the priority list when there's been a murder."

"OK. Thanks, Kevin. That's all good news. When we have the DNA, we may be able to identify the driver of the car, and he or she is almost certainly the person who set the fire. Have you anything back from her apartment?"

"Sorry, Sinéad was working on that. Shall I get her to give you a call?" Walsh said.

"Yes, please. But I think we should get someone over there again. There's more to be discovered I'm sure of it. Deirdre, can you arrange that for me?"

"Yes, sure. I think I'll go myself."

"Good idea. Oh, by the way, any word from Liam? He should be back by now," O'Shea said.

"I'll check when we are done here," Maguire said.

"OK. Thanks, Kevin. Let us know as soon as you have the DNA, and get Sinéad to call me."

"Right. I'll be off then. Talk later."

Walsh got up and left the room, leaving O'Shea and Maguire to ponder the new information. O'Shea was the first to ask the obvious question.

"What do your instincts tell you, Deirdre?"

"I think the McGroartys need to be looked into a bit further. Eoin was telling me that yer man has put in a claim for €10,000 for the damage to the parking area outside the camping site. The insurance company has rejected it, and he said that this wasn't the first time McGroarty had tried it on. And I wasn't too impressed with the missus either," Maguire said.

"I think the sooner you go and have a good root around at the apartment, the better," O'Shea said.

"I agree. I'll go first thing tomorrow."

"And there's something else. Do we have any phone records from this Maria at all? It should be easy enough to get her number from whatever advertising site she was using to attract the punters," O'Shea said.

"Good thinking. I'll put Liam on it as soon as I see him.

He must be developing a bit of a way with these young ladies!" Maguire said.

"Good idea. OK. Why don't you shoot off and get all that going? I'll talk to the super and see if I can calm him down a bit. At least we are making some progress at last - I think," O'Shea said.

"Right. I'll update you as soon as I have anything."

Maguire left her boss's office and went to see if Liam Staunton was back from his appointments. She found him at his desk in the open plan.

Chapter Eighteen

"Liam. You're back," Maguire said rather unnecessarily.

"Yes, Sarge."

"Well, how did you get on?"

"The first one was a bit useless. She didn't have anything of interest to say, but I had more luck with the second woman. Hanna is her name, and she was quite forthcoming. She told me that she thought Maria might have been involved with some gang or other who are trying to move in on the escort trade here. She even gave me a name, although she was a bit scared about that," Staunton said.

"Nice. Well, what's the name?"

"Roan Balla. She didn't have any other details, just the name. And before you ask, she didn't know what this Balla's involvement was. It's just that she heard it being mentioned in connection with the gang. The women talk to each other. They have a WhatsApp group."

"OK. Well, can you consult Professor Google and see if you can find anything on that name? Oh, and the boss wants you to see if you can find the ad that Maria used to attract her punters and get her phone number from it. We need to verify that Mrs Mac gave us the right one. Then, get onto the phone company and get the phone records for the last few weeks. Concentrate on incoming calls and see if you can identify anything that looks a bit out of place. Look at the timings carefully. We're looking for an incoming on the afternoon or evening she was killed." Maguire said.

"OK, Sarge. I might have to work late to cover all that. Is that OK?" Staunton said.

"Yes, of course. And let me know if you find anything of interest. I'm going out, but I'll be on my mobile," Maguire said.

Staunton turned to his PC. It was going to be a long night. But at the back of his mind was his earlier conversation with Hanna. He couldn't stop thinking about her.

* * *

Maguire decided not to leave it to the next day to visit Tober Hill. She drove straight there when she had left the Garda station. She pulled up outside Mrs McGroarty's apartments at number 22. The place looked to be empty, and there was still some evidence of the forensic team's work, with grey fingerprint powder on the front door frame and downstairs windows. But Maguire wasn't interested in that. She walked up to the front door of the adjoining property, number 20, and rang the bell.

As she waited, she could see the net curtains in the downstairs window twitching, and a few moments later, the door was answered by a short, elderly woman in a long floral print dress and a thin cream coloured cardigan on top. She had short, grey, almost white hair that was thinning remorselessly, and several dark liver spots on her face, which itself was wrinkled with age. Her hands were also wrinkled, and the joints on the one holding the door were enlarged, meaning that the woman had some form of arthritis.

"Yes?" she said, keeping the door almost closed.

"My name is Detective Sergeant Maguire from Westport," Maguire said, holding up her warrant card for the woman to inspect, "I wonder if I could ask you a few questions?"

"You'd better come in," the woman said, opening the door wider to admit Maguire.

The house she entered was not in anything like as good repair as Mrs McGroarty's place next door. Tired floral wallpaper adorned the walls in the narrow hallway, coming adrift near the ceiling where some ugly black mould had taken hold. The carpet was threadbare, and there was an unhealthy, musty smell throughout. The woman walked rather feebly to the back of the house, where a small kitchen with decor straight out of the 1960's was located. There was a dresser in green and cream with glass fronted doors on the top half, a Formica topped table, and three old chairs made with tubular steel frames and plastic seats, which were brittle and cracked in places. An old earthenware sink, with a wooden draining board and two very old brass taps, stood against the back window, which gave way to the rear garden, which was very overgrown and unkempt.

"Would you like a cup of tea, Sergeant?"

"No, thanks. I'm sorry, I didn't get your name."

"Bríd. Bríd McLoughlin. That's Mrs, although my husband is long gone. I live here on my own before you ask. What can I do for you, Sergeant?" Mrs McLoughlin said as she sat down at the table.

Maguire sat, too.

"I was wondering if you know anything about the house next door? Number 22," Maguire said.

"God in heaven, don't get me started. There does be fierce goings on in that place. Take my word for it."

"What sort of goings on?"

"It's occupied by women who seem to change every few weeks. And there's a string of men that come to the house at all hours. Five or six of them in a day. They stay for an hour or so and then leave again. I'm sure you can guess what that's all about," McLoughlin said, giving Maguire a knowing look.

"Do you ever get to talk to any of the women, Mrs McLoughlin?"

"I do not. What would I have to say to them? Dirty slags!"

"How long has this been going on?" Maguire asked.

"Ah, I don't keep track, Sergeant, but a couple of years anyway. Can you not do something about it? It's bringing down the neighbourhood something fierce."

Maguire ignored the question and pressed on with her enquiries.

"Can I ask you to cast your mind back to last week? It was probably Tuesday. Did you hear any kind of a row going on in there?"

"No, but there was something strange that happened around about then. I lose track of the days living here on my own, Sergeant. One day is much the same as the next," McLoughlin said.

"What was that?"

"Late on. I was just finished with the TV and was getting ready to go up. I saw a man coming out of the house, and he had a woman with him. He seemed to be supporting her or holding her up, like she was drunk. And you know I wouldn't be surprised if she was. Anyway, he helped her out onto the footpath, and they both got into an old black car and drove off," Mrs McLoughlin said.

"Would you recognize the man if you saw him again, Mrs McLoughlin?" Maguire said.

"Oh, no. I didn't get a look at his face at all. He was walking away from me, after all. But I can tell you he was around five foot eight inches tall, and he was wearing dark blue jeans and dark coloured running shoes."

"Do you mean trainers?"

"Well, whatever you call those things that all the young men wear these days. My father never wore anything but stout leather brogues, and they were always shiny and polished to perfection."

Maguire smiled, thinking of her own father, who was rarely seen without his rubber boots on. Except, of course, on Sundays when he went to mass. Then, he too wore shiny, polished black leather brogues.

"Do you think you might have seen this man visiting next door on a previous occasion?"

"I'm sorry. I couldn't say. There were so many men coming and going to that place. He might have been there before. I don't know."

"OK. Well, thanks Mrs McLoughlin. Our people will

still be working in number 22 a bit more tomorrow, but don't worry about it. That's been most helpful. We might need you to come down to the station to make a statement at some stage, but we'll send a car for you if needed. And don't worry. I think all that nonsense next door will come to an end now in any case."

"Well, that's something, I suppose."

Maguire got up from the table and made her way back to the door. Before she left, she bade goodbye to Mrs McLoughlin.

It was late afternoon by the time she had finished up at Tober Hill. She got back into her car, and the hands-free Bluetooth picked up Maguire's cell phone.

Before she started the engine, she called Eoin McNally. He answered after two rings.

"Hi, you. What are you up to?" McNally said.

"Nothing much. You?"

"Oh-oh. Sounds like you're in need of alcohol."

"You know me so well. Let me get home and have a shower. Pick me up at 7:30?"

"It's a date! And don't start drinking till I get there!"

She hung up.

Chapter Nineteen

Liam Staunton had been busy. He started by trying to verify the phone number that Maria had been using to attract clients while she was working in Westport. It wasn't straightforward because he rightly assumed that any advertisements that she had been using had expired, and hence were no longer available. But not all of the sites were fastidious, and after quite a while searching across them, he found an ad that could have been hers.

The ad was on Heartthrob.ie and outlined the services you might expect if you contacted Maria, and of course, helpfully, her phone number was provided. It was the same one that Mrs McGroarty had provided.

Staunton called the number, but it went to voicemail, where Maria advised in a sultry, almost whispering voice that she was probably working, urging the client to call back later for an unforgettable experience. Staunton didn't leave a message, but the call confirmed to him that the mobile phone was still alive, at least.

The airtime provider associated with Maria's phone was

Fone-a-Friend. The company didn't have a network of their own but rather piggybacked on one of the bigger Irish networks and bought airtime wholesale from them, selling it at a small margin.

Staunton looked up their website, which was festooned with all sorts of tempting offers, including all Irish calls, all texts, and all data for just €16 a month, provided you bought the handset from them. They guaranteed next day delivery anywhere in Ireland with the new phone and SIM card. There was a support number offered, and it seemed that their customer service was open from 9am to 6pm daily.

Staunton looked at the time on his own phone. It was 17:40, so he called the customer support line for Fone-a-Friend. The phone line clicked a few times, and then Staunton could hear a continental ringtone. After two rings, the call was answered.

"My name is Aisha; how can I help you today?" the woman said in what Staunton believed to be an Indian accent.

"Hello, Aisha. I'm with the Irish police. My name is Detective Garda Staunton. We need your help with something."

"Of course. What can we do?" Aisha said.

"I have a mobile phone number here, and I'm fairly sure that it is one of yours. Could you check that for me?"

"Yes, of course. What is the number?"

"It's 0846739200."

"Just a moment, I'll look it up for you. I'll just put you on hold for a minute."

Aisha went off the line, and Staunton was treated to

what he thought was probably Bollywood music. It had a low drumbeat and the sitar, and was very lively. After one repetition of the tune, Aisha was back.

"Hello, detective. Thank you for holding. Yes, that number is one of ours. I have the subscriber details here. Would you like me to call it out to you?"

"Yes, please."

"OK. The number belongs to Ms Maria Hyka. She has been a customer for almost a year."

"Excellent, Aisha. Thank you. How does Ms Hyka pay her bill?" Staunton said.

"It's paid by direct debit every month, and it's up to date. The last payment was last week."

"Good. I wonder if you could give me the bank account details where the bill is paid from, Aisha?"

"I don't have that here. But I can call a colleague in accounts and get it for you. But it might take a little while. Maybe I could email it to you later on?"

"Yes, OK, Aisha. And I'd also like to have the call records for the last month if that's possible?"

"Yes, OK, I can send that by email as well. What email should I use?" Aisha said.

"My email is liam.staunton@secure.garda.ie. Would you like me to spell that for you?"

"Just the first part with your name, please."

Staunton did as he was asked. He thanked Aisha for her help and ended the call. He hoped she would follow through with the information as she had said she would.

* * *

Staunton then turned his attention to the second task he had been assigned. This one was going to be significantly more difficult. He started by putting the name Roan Balla into Google. The search engine returned a number of hits, some of which even had photographs. But as Staunton went through them methodically, it soon became obvious that there were perfectly respectable citizens from a variety of different walks of life. Some were from Albania, but others apparently lived in either Montenegro or North Macedonia. He then turned his attention to the recently upgraded SIS system that connects law enforcement across Europe. The system contains alerts for people whom the police in various countries want to speak to, and is used to inform passport control officers and regular police of people to watch out for.

There was an alert for Roan Balla that originated in Croatia. There were very few details, but the Croatian police definitely had an interest in the man, focused on what was described simply as 'unauthorised activity'. Staunton made a note of the force that had placed the alert, but decided that there was no point in trying to contact anyone at this hour, as it was already well past closing time for offices in central Europe.

Staunton was about to pack up for the night when his PC pinged, indicating that he had received an email. He brought up his mail application and saw that the message was from Fone-a-Friend. Although he was keen to get out of the station - it had been a long day, and his eyes were hurting from staring at his PC for so long - he decided to open the message.

The email was from Aisha, whom he had spoken to earlier. It contained a PDF attachment with Maria Hyka's phone records going back over a month, and details of the bank account that was used to pay off the phone bill every month. Unfortunately, there was no address for Maria, but the bank sort code and branch address were shown, and to Staunton's surprise, the account was held in England with Northern Rock in Nottingham.

Staunton took the information and wrote a summary up on the whiteboard that had been set up in the open plan to try and bring the threads of the investigation together. Now if he could just find a way of getting a photograph of Maria Hyka, that would help the investigation considerably. Then he had an idea. But before he could act on it, his personal mobile phone started ringing on his desk. He didn't recognise the number, so he answered rather cautiously.

"Hello. Who's this, please?"

"Hi, Liam. This is Hanna. We met earlier. You asked me if I was free to have a drink with you. Are you still up for it?"

Staunton immediately recalled the way Hanna had kissed him when they met during the day, and her amazing beauty. He knew he probably shouldn't, but he said, "Yes, sure Hanna. Where would you like to meet?"

"Let's go to Lavery's pub. Do you know it?" Hanna said.

"Yes, of course. Shall we say twenty minutes?" Staunton said.

"Perfect. See you then."

"Yes, see you."

Chapter Twenty

The following morning, DS Deirdre Maguire was in early. She had spent a very enjoyable night with Eoin McNally, but he had to be at work by eight o'clock, so they had breakfasted together at 7am, and then both left Maguire's apartment and went their separate ways.

Maguire was studying the whiteboard with the additional information that Staunton had written up the previous night when he arrived in himself.

"Morning Sarge," he said, strolling over to where she was standing.

"Morning, Liam. Looks like you've been busy."

"Yes, I got the deceased's phone records yesterday evening and her bank details. Her real name is Maria Hyka, and strangely enough, her bank account is located in the United Kingdom. And I've been on to the passport people in Dublin and Shannon to see if I can get a scan of her passport from when she came in."

"Good work, Liam. Is there much data in the phone records?" Maguire said.

"About six pages of A4. Why?"

"I want you to go through it carefully. See if you can identify the last punter she was with or at least his phone number. But don't call it or anything. And then see if there are any other contacts of interest from this area. Let me know if you manage to find anything."

"Right, boss. Do you need a coffee?"

"Oh, great. Yes, please. Milk and one sugar please, Liam."

"Yes, I know Sarge," he said, smiling.

* * *

A few minutes later, DI Martin O'Shea arrived in the open plan.

"Morning all," he said cheerily, somewhat to the surprise of his team. O'Shea wasn't usually a morning person.

"When you have a minute, Deirdre, can we have a chat in my office?" he said.

"Yes, of course, boss. I'm right with you."

Just before Maguire went into O'Shea's office, Staunton handed her a cup of coffee, prepared just the way she liked it.

"You might need this, Sarge," he said with a conspiratorial grin.

"Thanks! I think!"

Once in O'Shea's office, Maguire took a seat in front of her boss's desk and placed her coffee down carefully on a beer mat. She looked expectantly at the man, waiting for him to speak.

"I was talking to the Super last night after you all went

home. He wants me to pursue this Roan Balla connection with the Europeans. And see what we can find. He would very much like this whole business to be down to some gangland feud involving foreigners. It's much easier to sell to the locals and the press. 'Eastern European gangs arrive in Westport' sort of thing," O'Shea said, tracing his hand across in front of his face, mimicking a newspaper headline.

"Do you think that's likely, boss?" Maguire said.

"It's certainly not out of the question, don't you agree?" O'Shea said, looking intently at his sergeant.

"Hmm .. I'm not so sure, boss. And I certainly don't think we have enough information yet to go flying kites with the press. If we're wrong, it would be very hard to row back on it. It could make us look like right eejits."

"I know, I know," O'Shea said rather impatiently, "don't worry, he's not going to go off half-cocked. But if it keeps him happy, who am I to argue?"

"That's all very well, sir, but the only thing we have implicating this Balla character - and it doesn't really implicate him at all - is that his name was written into a dead girl's notebook. We don't have any DNA or fingerprint evidence, and even if we had, what would we be able to compare it to?"

"That's my mission for today. I have to see if I can get that kind of thing from the European authorities. What are you up to?"

"I'm going back out with Kevin Walsh to Maria Hyka's rented rooms on Tober Hill. I want to do a really thorough search of her belongings. I think the place could have more to tell us," Maguire said.

"What is Liam doing?" O'Shea asked.

"He's going to analyse Maria's phone records and get onto her bank, which incidentally is in England. Nottingham, I think, he said. And he's getting a face pic from her passport scan at the airport when she entered the country too. That lot should get us an address for her at least, and a photograph of the girl."

"Excellent. OK. Let's get to it then. Let me know if you discover anything useful, won't you?"

"Yes, of course. And vice versa."

* * *

Maguire collected Kevin Walsh from forensics, and they drove the short distance to Tober Hill in Maguire's car. As the navigated the narrow streets, pulling in frequently to let traffic coming the other way past, Walsh asked, "What are you hoping to find out here, Deirdre?"

"Hopefully, something that will give us more information about the victim. We know very little about her, and if she was holed up here for a couple of weeks, she may have left something that could help us to identify her killer."

"Hmm .. maybe," Walsh said rather doubtfully.

When they arrived outside the property, Maguire pulled her car half up onto the footpath, so as not to obstruct the traffic too much. She noticed a big black Hyundai jeep parked on the other side of the street.

The two of them got out of the car and headed for the front door of number 22.

"That's odd," Maguire said, "the front door is open. Let's be careful."

Walsh and Maguire entered the property rather

tentatively. As they stopped in the hall, Mrs McGroarty appeared on the stairs carrying two black plastic bin bags that were evidently quite full.

"Mrs McGroarty, what are you doing?" Maguire said.

"I'm emptying that woman's stuff out of my apartment. I can't afford to leave it empty. I have a new tenant coming in later on for a week, and I need to have it ready," the woman said, struggling a little with her cargo as she descended the final few steps.

"Who told you that you could take Maria's stuff away?" Maguire said crossly.

"No one did. I don't need to be told. It's my house, after all."

"Mrs McGroarty, we are in the middle of a murder investigation. What you have, there may be material evidence. You shouldn't have disturbed the place like that. We haven't finished examining it yet."

Maguire gestured to Walsh to go upstairs and see what was left in the apartment that might be of interest if anything. Then she turned her attention back to Mrs McGroarty.

"What's in the bags?"

"Just her clothes and some personal bits and bobs. Nothing much."

"Right, well, I'll be having those then, thank you," Maguire said.

"You can't take it. It's not your stuff. There's bedlinen that belongs to the apartment in here."

Maguire had had enough of this.

"Much of it isn't yours either, Mrs McGroarty. Now, hand it over before I do you for obstruction, and I can tell you, we don't appreciate what you have done here. You may be hearing more about it when I tell my DI."

Mrs McGroarty thrust the two bags in Maguire's direction. She had a face like thunder on her, but she said no more. She just stomped out the door and back to her car.

Upstairs, Walsh was looking around the place when Maguire joined him.

"What's the story, Liam?"

"She's done a right number on it. Not a trace of poor Maria to be found, and it's all made up, ready for the new arrival."

"Bugger. O'Shea won't be best pleased. OK, let's get out of here. We're not going to find anything."

They drove back in silence to the Garda station.

As Maguire was walking back into the building, having left Liam Walsh off, her phone rang.

"Maguire," she answered.

She listened to what the caller had to say in almost complete silence, eventually broken when she said, "I see. Well, thank you for telling me," and she hung up.

Chapter Twenty-One

Back inside the Garda station, Maguire found Staunton on the telephone, with his PC screen showing a page from Northern Rock's site. When he saw her, he put his hand over the mouthpiece and said in a low whisper, "I'm just holding on listening to radio ga-ga. Did you want me?"

"When you're finished, come and find me."

Maguire went to her own desk, and started reading her emails, but she was unable to concentrate. The phone call she received a few minutes earlier had disturbed her, and she wanted an opportunity to clear the air.

A few minutes later, Liam Staunton came across to her desk and pulled up a chair.

"Hi, boss. I've dug up a few things that could be of interest, but I can't quite figure it all out."

"What's that then, Liam?" she said, rather more cooly than she wanted to.

"It's Maria Hyka's phone records. There are quite a few exchanges between her mobile and an Irish number. They go back well before she allegedly came here, as in several months. And the thing is, the number she was in touch with belongs to Mrs McGroarty."

"Bloody hell. Are you sure, Liam?"

"Yes. I am. I called it just to check, and it was her all right. No doubt."

"So, let's just be clear; Maria Hyka was in regular touch with Mrs McGroarty for some time before she rented her apartment out at Tober Hill?" Maguire said.

"Yes. Looks like it. And there's more. Mrs McGroarty's new tenant that she was so keen to have the place ready for is a single Eastern European woman."

"I see. I think it's time that we had another word with the good landlady, don't you?"

"Yes, but maybe we should box a bit clever, boss," Staunton said.

"How do you mean?"

"Why don't we start with her husband? See if we can get him to tell us a bit about what's going on."

"Hmm .. not a bad idea, Liam. Are you up for it?"

"Yes, of course," Staunton said.

"But let me make a phone call first. We might have a bit more to talk to him about! Give me a minute. I'll come and get you."

"Right, Sarge."

Maguire called Eoin McNally.

"Hi. It's me. Listen, you know we were talking about that McGroarty chap that runs the caravan and camping site out at Bertra Beach?"

"Yes, of course."

"Well, we're just about to go out and interview him

about something. But I need a bit of information first. What's happening with his €10,000 claim for damage to the car park?"

"Ah. As you know, we rejected the claim. Then, I arranged for us to get three separate estimates from local contractors to restore the area to pristine condition. That meant laying some new blacktop over the damage, and re white-lining the spaces. The most expensive one we got was for €2,600, and the cheapest was €1,700. So, he was definitely trying it on."

"That's great, Eoin. I won't let you know how we found out, but it will definitely give us some leverage. Thanks," Maguire said.

"Are you around later on?"

"Yes, should be. Do you want to meet up?"

"I'd love to," McNally said.

"Tell you what. Why don't I cook? Nothing fancy. Just a five-course dinner with haute cuisine at mine, at say eight o'clock. You bring the plonk. Nothing cheap, mind you. OK?"

"So, that will be Chinese take-away then," he said.

"Cheeky bugger! Go on. I'll see you later!"

* * *

It was a bright afternoon as they drove out towards the beach. Maguire glanced out to sea when the R335 met the coast just short of Murrisk. The ocean was a deep aquamarine colour, and sea birds were soaring and swooping over the bay, occasionally diving into the water and coming up again with a small fish in their beaks.

As they passed Murrisk, Maguire said to Staunton, "Liam, I need to talk to you about something."

"Yes, Sarge, what is it?"

"Were you out on a date last night with one of the escort girls? And don't bother denying it. You were seen."

"It was nothing, boss. Just a drink."

"Christ Liam! Are you out of your mind?"

"It was nothing. Really. When I interviewed her, she took my card, and she rang me after and asked if we could meet for a drink. I thought she might have more evidence to share, so I agreed," Staunton said.

"Yeah, right. And I'm bloody Lady Godiva. Jesus, Liam, what were you thinking of? If a brief got to hear of this, our whole case could be compromised. Please tell me you didn't sleep with this, Hanna, or whatever her name is."

"Yes, it's Hanna, and no, I didn't sleep with her. What do you take me for?"

"A bloody idiot right now, Liam. That's what."

Staunton didn't say anything for quite some time, but then he found his voice again.

"Will the DI have to know?"

"He will. And you're going to tell him what's more. As soon as we get back to the station."

Staunton fell silent again.

Maguire pulled the car into the car park at the Bertra Bay camping and caravan site. They both got out, and were met by a salty fresh breeze blowing in off the Atlantic.

"God, the air is good out here," Maguire said to no one in particular.

The two of them went in through the gates and walked up to the office, which was itself an adapted pale green mobile home. They climbed into the office and found Gerry McGroarty seated behind a desk at the far end of the unit. He stood as they entered.

"Good morning, folks. How can I help you today?" McGroarty said.

"Good morning, Mr McGroarty," Maguire said, "can you confirm that you have put in a claim on your insurance policy for €10,000 with regard to damage to the car park resulting from the fire where the young woman was burnt."

McGroarty looked suspiciously at Maguire, and came round the desk to stand quite closely in front of her.

"That's a civil matter, Sergeant. What's it got to do with you?"

"No, Mr McGroarty. It's fraudulent, and that's a police matter."

She waited for this to sink in. McGroarty was looking rather apprehensive before Maguire went on, "But that's not why we are here. Not this time, anyway. What do you know about the rental apartments that your wife has up on Tober Hill?"

"How do you mean?" McGroarty said.

"Are you aware that the premises is being used by foreign escort girls to ply their seedy trade?"

McGroarty advanced on Maguire and gripped her upper arms tightly.

"Now listen here, you. You can't go making wild statements like that, accusing my good lady of God knows what. You have no right!"

McGroarty was angry now, with a little spittle issuing from his lips as he spoke, and he had gone very red in the face.

Staunton stepped forward and said in a very firm tone, "Release my colleague immediately, Mr McGroarty, or I will book you for assaulting a police officer to add to your troubles."

McGroarty looked to Staunton and saw the determination in his eyes. He let go of Maguire's arms.

"So, let's be having it, Mr McGroarty. What is your wife doing with those apartments? And it would be a very bad idea to hold anything back. You're in enough trouble as it is."

"You're the detectives. You figure it out," McGroarty said, and turned his back on them.

Maguire looked at Staunton, who just shrugged.

"Come on, Liam. Let's get out of here," Maguire said, and turned once again to McGroarty, "You haven't heard the last of this, Mr McGroarty. Obstructing the Gardaí is a serious matter." But the man didn't respond, so the detectives just left.

"Where to now, boss?" Staunton said when they were back in the car.

"Let's head back to the office. You have your confessional with the DI, and I want to follow up on something before we see Mrs Mc again."

Chapter Twenty-Two

Back at the Garda station, Staunton went off to see if he could find DI O'Shea to tell him about his meeting with Hanna the previous night. He was grateful that Maguire had left him to tell the story. That way, he felt he could paint the encounter as totally innocent and hope to avoid any kind of sanction.

Maguire called Kevin Walsh in the forensic laboratory.

"Hi, Kevin. It's Deirdre Maguire. I was just wondering if you have any results back on the DNA from the sticking plaster that was found in the car?"

"Hang on a sec, I'll have a look for you," Walsh said.

He put down the phone, and Maguire could hear him tapping out something on his computer keyboard.

"Hello, Deirdre? Are you there?" he said a few moments later.

"Yes, what have you got?"

"I can't quite believe it. The DNA from the little plaster is a close familial match to the victim, or so it says here. There's about a 50% correlation."

"How do you mean, Kevin?" Maguire said, not quite understanding the information that she was hearing.

"Well, the blood on the plaster isn't hers. It's from someone closely related to her - probably a sibling."

"But that doesn't make any sense, Kevin. Are you sure there hasn't been a mistake?

"This science doesn't lie, Deirdre. If you want, I can have it run again, but I guarantee you'll get exactly the same result, and it will be expensive, too."

"Blimey! That's a turn-up for the books. Is the sample from the plaster male or female?" Maguire said.

"Male. Definitely a man, so very likely it's from her brother."

"And you're sure that it couldn't be hers and just got mucked up in the fire?"

"No chance. We found the sticking plaster right down by the outside of the driver's seat, by the door. The victim was never in the driver's seat, from what we were able to establish. And anyway, then the DNA would be a 100% match to her," Walsh said.

"OK. Thanks, Liam. I'm not sure where that leaves us, but thanks for the information, anyway. Bye."

* * *

Liam Staunton was a bright young detective, but he needed to paint an innocent picture to DI O'Shea about his meeting with Hanna the previous evening. He decided to box a bit cleverly. He knocked a little tenuously on the DI's door.

"Come in," O'Shea responded from within.

"Hello, boss, got a minute?"

"Yes, sure, Liam, come in, grab a seat. What's on your mind?"

"I've managed to get hold of Maria Hyka's bank records from Northern Rock, sir. And they gave me her address in Nottingham as well. They were a bit reluctant, but I managed to wheedle it out of them after a few minutes," Staunton said.

"That's good work, Liam. Well done. I'll have a chat with DS Maguire in a little while, and see how she wants to play it."

"Yes, OK, boss, but I haven't told her yet. I thought I'd bring it to you first."

O'Shea looked suspiciously at the young officer.

"C'mon, Liam. Out with it. What are you really here for?" O'Shea said. He hadn't been a detective for many years without being able to smell a rat.

Staunton went a bit red in the face, and looked down into his lap before replying.

"DS Maguire wanted me to tell you that I met one of the call girls for a drink last night, boss. I wanted to see if she could give us any more information about the case. After all, she gave us the name of this Balla character."

"And I don't suppose this woman is an ugly old bat with a squint and a limp, Liam. Am I right?"

"No, sir. She's lovely looking. But we didn't do anything. We just talked for a while in the pub. That's all. Honestly."

O'Shea thought for a moment before replying.

"Well, I don't suppose it's a hanging offence, Liam. But DS Maguire was right to get you to tell me about it, and I would strongly advise that if you need to speak to her again, you are accompanied and do it during working hours. Is that clear?"

"Yes, of course, sir. Thank you," Staunton said, cheering up noticeably.

"Is that all, Liam?"

"Yes, sir."

"Right. And that was good work with Maria Hyka's address."

Staunton got up and made for the door, greatly relieved that the DI had been so understanding. But as he went back to his desk in the open plan, he couldn't help but recall Hanna's warmth, with her amazing blue eyes, pretty face, and a terrific body.

* * *

DS Maguire was next to knock on DI O'Shea's door. She went in without being asked, but that was standard procedure between the two of them, who worked very closely together.

Hi, boss," she said, "got a minute?"

"Yes, sure, Deirdre. Take a seat. What's up?"

Maguire told the DI about the information that Kevin Walsh had provided about the DNA sample from the sticking plaster. O'Shea was surprised by the news but reacted calmly.

"I see. Well, that puts a whole new perspective on the whole thing, doesn't it?" he said.

"Yes, it does. Quite a surprise, to be honest. And I don't

know what it means for the Balla bloke either. That could just be a red herring."

O'Shea thought for a few moments before speaking again.

"OK. Let's get the team together. Did Liam tell you that he has an address in Nottingham for Maria Hyka?"

"Yes, he mentioned it after he's been in to see you. What did he want, by the way?"

"Nothing much. Just some nonsense about one of the escort girls. I warned him off. Told him not to be an idiot. Good call, incidentally, getting him to tell me himself," O'Shea said.

"Ah, I don't think it's a problem, but better to have it out in the open, at least. I imagine that'll be the end of it. I'll go and set up a briefing. Shall we say ten minutes?"

"Yes, fine. Thanks."

Chapter Twenty-Three

The team assembled a few minutes later in the open plan. DI O'Shea came out of his office and took a seat in front of them all.

"Right, folks. There have been some developments that are material to the Maria Hyka case. Thanks to Liam here, we now have an address for her in Nottingham, and DS Maguire has discovered that there was forensic material from the car that indicates a close family relation may have been driving it before it was set alight."

Agnes Gallagher looked at Liam Staunton with a puzzled expression. O'Shea continued to address the group.

"So, there may be parents or other relations in Nottingham who have no idea that their daughter has been murdered, and if there is a brother living with them, he is most certainly a person of interest to us. I suggest that we sideline any further enquiries on this Balla character, and see if we can get in touch with the parents, if they are actually in Nottingham. It's not a common name, so they may not be too hard to find."

Maguire put her hand up, and O'Shea acknowledged it.

"Yes, Deirdre, go ahead."

"What about the McGroartys, boss?"

"I think they'll keep for a while. Let's try to get to the bottom of the killing first, and then we can deal with them. They aren't going anywhere," O'Shea said.

"OK. So, what do we do about the Nottingham connection?" Maguire asked.

"That's a bit tricky, Deirdre. I don't imagine the UK plod will be too interested frankly, but we can't just go over there and start stomping around on their patch, causing mayhem without them being advised. Would you be willing to travel across if I can find a way to square it with the UK police?"

"I suppose so, boss. Could I bring someone with me?"

"Let's see what I can arrange. I'll have to go upstairs and talk to Superintendent O'Connell and see what he has to say about it. Meantime, Liam, can you do a proper root around and see if you can get any further information on the Hyka family in Nottingham? And, Deirdre, could you travel at short notice if it comes to that?"

"Yes, sir, that wouldn't be a problem."

"Good. Now, while we are at it, someone needs to go back out to Kenny's Karz and talk to Jim Kenny again. We need him to be a bit more forthcoming about the person who bought the car from him. I think if we lean on him a bit, he may open up. Volunteers?"

Agnes Gallagher put up her hand.

"I can do that, sir. The others are fairly busy," she said.

"Are you sure you are up to it, Agnes? I imagine Kenny can be tough enough," O'Shea said.

"You haven't seen me in action, boss. Don't worry. If he has any information, I'll get it out of him."

"All right, then. You're on. I'll go and see the Super and try and fix something up for the UK. Let's get together again later."

* * *

The group broke up, and as Liam Staunton was walking back to his desk, his personal mobile phone began to ring and vibrate in his pocket. He took it out and recognised the number immediately.

"Hi, Hanna," he said softly into the device. He looked around rather furtively to see if he was being observed, but no one was paying any attention to him.

"Hello, policeman Liam. Can you talk?" Hanna said.

"Hold on a moment, I'll move to somewhere quieter."

Staunton moved out of the open plan office to the corridor where he couldn't be overheard.

"OK, Hanna. This is better. How are you?"

"I'm good. I just wanted to call you to say that I am leaving tomorrow evening and going back home. I have had a very good time here, and I have made enough money to keep Johann and my mother for a good few months. I was wondering if I could see you tonight before I go, Liam?"

"Oh, it's a bit awkward, Hanna. I'd love to meet you, but last time we were out in the pub, some nosey person saw us and told my sergeant. She was furious because the case we are working on could be compromised."

"I'm sorry, Liam. I didn't mean to get you into trouble. But you could come around here to mine, maybe after dark.

I don't mind how late it is. I just want to see you before I go. Please."

Staunton was torn between his duty as a Garda and his desire to be with this beautiful young woman one more time before she walked out of his life forever.

"OK. Listen. I'll come around at eleven o'clock. The street will be quiet then. I'll ring the bell twice, and you can let me in quickly so that I am not seen. Is that OK?"

"Yes. Thanks. I'll see you later."

* * *

Superintendent Derry O'Connell was in relatively good humour when DI O'Shea knocked on his door.

"Come in, Martin. How's things?"

O'Shea entered the room and took a seat opposite the superintendent, who was seated at rather a large walnut reproduction partner's desk with a red leather top. The desk was almost clear, save for two telephones and a rack of three bright red stationery trays, bulging with several overstuffed manilla folders.

"We're making progress, sir," and O'Shea went on to fill his boss in on the latest developments in the case of the Maria Hyka murder.

"I was wondering, sir, if you might have any contacts in the Nottinghamshire Police?" O'Shea said.

"God, you picked the right spot there, Martin. How do you do it? As it happens, I have a good contact in Nottingham. His name is William Bennett, Billy to his friends. He used to be a Garda inspector in Galway, but he fell in love with an English rose, and emigrated to

Nottingham. I think he's a DCI now. He's always asking me to go over for a cricket match at Trent Bridge."

"Do you think he'd be OK if a couple of us went over to follow up with Maria's family? We think there may be a brother that may somehow have been involved, and of course, there's her parents too, who probably don't know that their daughter is dead."

"Well, I can certainly give Billy a call and see how the land lies. It might be best if we could keep it below the radar, as it were. Things can get very complicated if we have to go down the official route. When do you want to do this?" O'Connell said.

"As soon as it can be arranged, if that's OK, sir?"

"All right. Leave it with me, and I'll get back to you later."

Chapter Twenty-Four

Agnes Gallagher drove out to the Ballinrobe Road, where Jim Kenny plied his dubious trade. She pulled her car up in front of a smart, and quite new, Nissan X-trail, which she rightly assumed was what Kenny was driving. It was a very superior vehicle to the bangers he was inflicting on his gullible customers.

Off to the side, parked on the grass, there was a small collection of elderly cars with paper stuck inside the windscreens advertising the sale price of the jalopies, the most expensive of which was €999.

Gallagher got out of her car and walked up the short path to the door of Kenny's house, which she found open. There was a distinct aroma of fried food emanating from the hallway. She stood on the doorstep and called inside.

"Hello. Mr Kenny. Are you there?"

She could hear the sound of a wooden chair scraping against the floor in the kitchen, which was at the back of the house, and a moment later, the large, untidy figure of Jim

Kenny came into view, holding a knife and fork. When he saw Gallagher, he broke into a smile.

"Hello, Miss. Are you looking to get yourself a car? I have a nice wee Ford Fiesta out there that would suit you grand. Dead cheap too," Kenny said.

Gallagher held up her warrant card. When Kenny saw it, his demeanour changed radically, and he snarled, "Ah, what do you lot want this time? Can't you see I'm at my food?"

"As you know, Mr Kenny, we are investigating a murder, and I need you to answer a few questions about the man who bought the black Toyota Avensis from you."

"I've told the others that were here all I know. Now, why don't you get lost and leave me in peace?" Kenny said. He turned his back on Gallagher and started walking back down the hall.

Gallagher wasn't to be put off so easily. She entered the house and followed the man into the kitchen. When Kenny saw her, he said, "I don't remember inviting you in, missy."

"That's Detective Garda Gallagher to you, Mr Kenny. And as I said, I need to ask you some questions. It won't take long, and then you'll be able to get back to your meal."

Kenny didn't respond. He just stood there trying to look menacing, so Gallagher went on.

"I want you to tell me as much as you can remember about the buyer of that Toyota. What kind of accent did he have?"

Kenny shrugged. "Just ordinary. Maybe a bit of English in it somewhere, but nothing special."

"How long was he here?"

"I dunno. About twenty minutes, I guess."

"And are you sure he didn't leave a name, or tell you anything about who he was, or where he was from?"

"I told those other two. No, he didn't. And to be honest, Detective Garda Gallagher, I'm not sure I like your line of questioning. I've done nothing wrong, and you're not welcome here. So, I'd like you to leave."

Gallagher had had enough of this nonsense. She walked over to where Kenny was seated once again in front of a greasy fry.

"Mr Kenny. If I had a mind to, I could arrest you here and now on a number of charges relating to your so-called car dealership. You have violated several regulations, and I'm sure if we went to the trouble of checking out all the vehicles you have traded over the past, say, two years, we'd find one or two at least of dubious provenance. So, I'd advise you to cooperate."

Kenny stood up from the table, still holding his knife and fork out in front of him, and approached Gallagher. But she was too quick for him.

"Go on, Jim. Just try it, and then I'll be able to add assaulting a Garda to the list of charges!"

Gallagher retreated and sat down again.

"All right. Enough! But I don't think I can help. Honestly."

"Think back. Did he give you any idea what he was about, or where he had come from, or what he was doing here?"

Kenny thought for a moment, and then said, "Well, he did ask me where he might find a girl in Westport. I told him he was asking the wrong person, but then he said he would be willing to pay. So, I told him to go into town to that internet place where he found the car advertised and do a search. He seemed happy with that, then we did the business with the car, and he left in it."

"Right. Well, it's a pity you didn't tell my colleagues that the first time. Now, is there anything else that might have slipped your mind?"

"No. That's it. Now, can you leave me in peace to finish me bleeding dinner?"

"For now, Mr Kenny, for now."

Gallagher turned on her heels and left the house, happy with her work, and glad to be getting away from the stink of greasy food.

* * *

DI O'Shea was getting ready to leave the station for the day when his desk phone rang.

"Ah, Martin, I'm glad I caught you," Superintendent O'Connell said when O'Shea picked up. "I managed to get hold of Billy Bennett. He's only after getting a promotion to superintendent, hasn't he, the rogue. Anyway, he said he can provide a couple of your finest with a bit of cover for a few days if you want to send them over. He said to tell them not to go throwing their weight about, but if they act discreetly, it should be OK, and he gave me his personal number in case they run into trouble."

"Oh, great, sir. Thanks very much for organising that," O'Shea said.

"Who are you going to send?" O'Connell said.

"DS Maguire, plus one, sir. I haven't worked out the full details yet."

"Oh, right. Well, give me both names when you have them, and be sure to tell them that this is all very unofficial, so they'll have to be careful how they operate. And be sure to keep me informed."

"Of course, sir. And thanks again."

Chapter Twenty-Five

The evening had turned quite chilly. It was overcast, but there was definitely a change in the weather, and not for the better. It wasn't raining, but Staunton knew the signs. The rain would be along soon, and then the temperature would fall even more.

Still, it suited his purpose. As he drew up outside the premises where Hanna was staying, the street was deserted. He parked his car quite a long way past the building, and sat inside with the engine and lights off just observing for several minutes. Content that he wasn't being watched, he set the interior light in his car to remain off as he opened the door, and got out. Once outside, he did a quick scan again to make sure that there was no one around, and crossed the road to Hanna's door. He jabbed the doorbell twice and waited. It was five past eleven.

He could hear footsteps coming down the stairs, and a moment later Hanna opened the door. Once again, Staunton was struck by the awesome beauty of this woman. Her blonde hair was tied back in a pony tail, and she had just the right amount of makeup on her face. She reached out and took Staunton's hand, and led him indoors.

Before they ascended the stairs, Hanna faced Staunton and reached up to draw him to her. She kissed him softly on the lips as he put his arms around her. He felt he was in heaven.

When they got to Hanna's flat, she had a bottle of good red wine already opened, and had a few small snacks set out on the table. She sat at one of the kitchen chairs, and Staunton took the other.

As she poured a generous measure of the wine for her visitor, she said, "Well, Liam. How are things going with you?"

"Oh, I can't complain. The cased is moving along, but of course, I can't discuss it, for obvious reasons."

"No, of course not. And I haven't heard anything more about poor Maria either. I guess it will have to remain a mystery."

"So, Hanna, you are leaving us, is that right?" Staunton said.

"Yes. I must go back home. My mother and Johann need the money I have earned, and I'm longing to see them. I don't like to be away for too long. Johann is growing up so quickly."

"Yes. It must be difficult for you. How did you get into this line of work anyway?"

Hanna looked at him and smiled broadly.

"Always the policeman, eh, Liam? But it's not difficult. Many women my age do this type of work. It pays well, and if you can stay out of the hands of the gangs, you get to keep what you earn. I confess, Liam, we don't pay tax!"

Staunton laughed at that.

"But do you think it's safe, Hanna?" he said.

"For me, yes. I know I don't look very tough, but believe me, I can handle myself if someone decided to get rough. A man with no clothes on is very vulnerable in certain parts of his anatomy!"

"I see what you mean. So how do you think Maria got herself into such trouble then?" Staunton said.

"Who knows? Maybe she was taken by surprise, or perhaps the attacker had a weapon of some kind. It's hard to tell without knowing more," Hanna said.

"I'm sorry, love, I really can't say anything about the case."

"It's OK. I'm just a bit curious, that's all."

Staunton was keen to change the subject.

"So, when are you actually leaving, Hanna?"

"Tomorrow evening. I will get the last bus that goes directly to Dublin airport, and then I'll spend the night there because my flight is very early on Saturday morning. I fly directly to Prague, and then it's another bus to my town. It's about an hour."

"Wow! That's a lot of travelling. And I don't like the idea of you having to spend the night at the airport. Could you not get a hotel, or maybe a guest house?" Staunton said.

"No. I will be too late, and anyway, it's only a few hours."

Staunton thought for a moment.

"What time does your flight actually depart, Hanna?"

"It's at 7.15am, so I'll check in at 5.30 and get some breakfast. I don't like the food on the plane."

"I have a better idea, Hanna. Why don't I drive you? It's

about three hours door to door, so we could go at, say, 2.30 to leave time in case we get a puncture, but I'd have you there in good time."

Hanna got up and came over to where Staunton was sitting, and sat down on his lap.

"You are a really lovely guy, Liam. Would you really do that for me? I can pay for your petrol," she said.

"No, you won't, Hanna. I am doing this for a friend. And friends don't do that. I'd be happy to drive you. And it means I get to be with you a bit longer," he said, smiling at her.

Hanna bent forward and kissed Staunton again. He could feel the warmth of her body against his, and it was driving him wild. Before things got out of hand, he decided he needed to go.

When they had stopped kissing, Staunton gently eased Hanna off his lap.

"I'd better get going, Hanna. Otherwise, I won't be able to leave at all."

"Would that be so bad?"

"Yes, Hanna, it would. I would lose my job. I'm sorry. It's not that I don't want to stay; of course, I do, but we have to be sensible."

"Tell you what, Liam. Why don't you come around earlier tomorrow? Then we can be together for a few hours before we set off. Is that OK?"

"Hmm, yes, I think that would be OK. Maybe if I got here at ten o'clock. Would that be all right?" Staunton said.

"Yes, perfect. But do you really have to go now?"

"Yes, I'd better. But I'll see you soon. Are you working tomorrow, Hanna?"

"No. I need to pack, and clean this place up. Anyway, I've done enough work on this trip. I need a break."

They kissed a bit more before Staunton finally, reluctantly, disengaged. He left not knowing whether he was doing the right thing, or not.

Chapter Twenty-Six

The following morning, DI O'Shea called Maguire into his office.

"OK, Deirdre, we have the go ahead to visit Maria's family in Nottingham. Can you get on and make the arrangements? I think it would be good if you could travel tomorrow. It's the weekend, and you are more likely to find the Hykas in."

"Yes, OK, boss. Am I going on my own?" Maguire said.

"No. I think it would be much better if there were two of you."

"So, who's going with me then?"

"I think it would be best if you took Agnes with you. Two female officers are less threatening, and you'll slip under the radar with the local plod more easily. Are you happy with that?"

"Yes, sure. We'll probably have to hire a car. I think East Midlands is the nearest airport, and then Nottingham isn't very far away."

"Great. Well, off you go and make the arrangements. I

have to tell the super who's travelling so he can square it with his mate over there. He knows another superintendent that used to work here, it seems, Billy Bennett, I think he said. Make a note of that name in case you need it."

"OK, thanks, boss. Do you want to tell Agnes, or shall I?"

"No, leave that to me. In fact, could you ask her to pop into me now?"

"Yes, sure."

A few minutes later Agnes Gallagher was fully briefed by DI O'Shea. She was pleased to be selected for this mission, which, as had been pointed out by the senior officer, was a tad delicate in nature. But she also wondered what they might discover on the trip to the United Kingdom. Would they discover why Maria Hyka had been so cruelly disposed of, and could it really be a blood relative that had done the evil deed?

When Gallagher got back to the open plan, she went over to where Maguire was seated at her desk, busy on the PC.

"Hi, boss. The DI gave me the good news. What are you looking at?" Gallagher said.

"Hi, Agnes. I'm just doing a lookup on Google maps to get our bearings for the visit. The address we have is Barton Road, Nottingham, and as far as I can see, it's on the south side of the city off Radcliffe Road. I had a look at Street View, too. The Hyka's house looks like a 1940's or 50's semi-detached in good order. I don't imagine we'll encounter too much trouble, but it's best to be prepared, just in case. I hope you hadn't planned anything exciting for the weekend?" Maguire said.

"Oh, just a quick trip to Las Vegas to gamble away my life savings, but it's nothing that won't keep," Gallagher said, smiling.

"Great. Now our flight is early on Saturday, so why don't I pick you up at say 5am. We should be at the airport by around eight, and that'll give us time to get some breakfast before the flight."

"Yeah, sounds about right. What time does it take off?"

"9.50am, and it's Ryanair, so I'll book two seats together near the front. Just bring one carry-on bag, and I'll do the same. OK?" Maguire said.

"Yes, fine. And I'll have my driving license too in case we want to share the driving."

"Great. Now leave me in peace to get all this organised. I'll have to get some sterling cash from somewhere, too. Why couldn't they use the Euro like the rest of us?" Maguire said out loud, but Gallagher was already away.

Gallagher went back to her desk and started to go over all the evidence that they had in the case of Maria Hyka, deceased. She focused her attention on the DNA results that implicated a close relative to the killing. Surely this wasn't right. But she told herself that science doesn't lie, and that meant that she and her boss might be about to run into a murderer, in a strange country, with no backup. 'Terrific' she thought to herself.

* * *

Maguire arrived outside Gallagher's house the following morning at just before five o'clock. It was quite bright by that time, and Gallagher had no trouble spotting her arrival. She joined Maguire in the car.

"Morning, boss. Nice day for it."

When Gallagher was settled with her seat belt fastened, Maguire set off.

"OK, Agnes, from now on, it's only first names. No 'boss' or 'sarge'. We're just two women off for a weekend break in the UK. OK?"

"Yes, sure, boss, eh .. sorry, Deirdre. I'll get the hang of it soon, don't worry. Let's hope we don't end up like Thelma and Louise!"

Maguire laughed.

"Let's hope not!"

They drove on for some time in companionable silence. It was a fine day, with just a few high clouds drifting slowly across the country. There had been some rain overnight, but it had cleared away to the east, and the roads were almost dry again.

When they got past Frenchpark approaching Strokestown, Maguire said, "Would you like to stop for a coffee or something, Agnes?"

"No, I'm OK thanks, unless you would like to. And by the way, I can do some of the driving if you're feeling tired or whatever."

"Thanks. Maybe further on, but I'm good for the moment. So, tell me, Agnes, what's going on in your world just now?"

"As in?"

"As in social life, family, boyfriends, or girlfriends?" Maguire said.

"Well, you can forget girlfriends, Deirdre, for starters."

"Sorry. But you never know these days, and it doesn't matter to me anyway."

"I don't have a particular boyfriend just now. The job doesn't really lend itself to long-term relationships, does it?"

"No. It's difficult," Maguire said.

"But you have a boyfriend, don't you?"

"Yes, I suppose so. Actually, I should say yes. Eoin is quite attentive and very thoughtful. I'm pretty fond of him, but don't say I said!"

"I'm just a sad bachelorette for now, I'm afraid."

"Never mind. You're still very young. But what about Liam? He's an eligible sort of chap," Maguire said.

"My dad told me ages ago when I joined the Guards that I should never mix work and play. So even if I fancied him, which I don't by the way, he's out of bounds for me. What about you and the DI?"

"Not on your life. He's married for heaven's sake. And as you said, work and play. Hey, look! Isn't that Liam Staunton's car going the other way?"

Gallagher looked out the passenger window, but the car Maguire was referring to had gone past. Maguire hastily reached up behind the rear-view mirror and hit the red button on her dash camera.

"There. That will ensure the clip is preserved. We can look at it later. But I'm sure that was Liam Staunton, and it's the same type of car that he drives. I wonder what in God's name he's doing coming back to Westport at this time of day. And where has he been?" Maguire said.

"Hmm .. curious OK. But hardly sinister. We can ask him when we get back from England."

Chapter Twenty-Seven

The flight from Dublin to East Midlands Airport was on time and uneventful. Maguire had booked two seats near the front of the cabin, and at this early hour on a Saturday, the flight was not very full, so the third seat in the row was empty, allowing them to take the window and aisle seat and leave the middle one vacant.

The two detectives collected their hire car from the Hertz desk. They were given a Nissan Qashqai, which was almost brand new and very comfortable.

Gallagher got the sat-nav going and input the address that they had for the Hyka household, and they set off. Their route took them around Kegworth, then along the A453 to Barton and Clifton, before they turned off to the right to skirt the south side of the city and bring them to their destination. Before they arrived at the house, Maguire pulled the car into a disused gateway.

"Right, Agnes, we need to agree on how this goes down. Apart from informing the Hykas about the death of their daughter, although, of course, they may already know, we need to see if we can get a fix on their son, and that could be a bit tricky. I suggest we try and split them up. Are you OK with that?"

"Yes, of course, Deirdre. I'll take the woman if that's all right and leave you with himself," Gallagher said.

"Yes, OK. Is there anything else you want to sort out before we go in?"

"No, I guess we'll have to largely play it by ear. I hope I'll be OK."

"You'll be fine, don't worry. Let's go."

The two Garda detectives got out of their hired car and walked through the garden to the front door. The house was very well kept, with the grass neatly cut and the flowerbeds along the edge of the driveway completely free of weeds. The front door was a partially glazed wooden panel affair which looked to be original. A modern electric doorbell was screwed to the frame on the left hand side, and Maguire pressed it. They could hear the shrill ringing deep inside the house.

A couple of minutes later, they could see a shape through the glass part of the door, and it was opened wide by a slim woman with wavy grey hair wearing a cream blouse and grey skirt well below the knee.

"Yes. How can I help you?" the woman said in a slightly foreign accent.

Maguire addressed the lady.

"Good morning. Mrs Hyka?"

"Yes. Who are you?"

"My name is Deirdre Maguire, and this is my friend

Agnes Gallagher. I wonder if we could have a word with you and your husband? We have come from Ireland."

The woman looked rather curiously at the two of them, and said, "Well, I suppose you'd better come in then."

Mrs Hyka stood back and ushered the two detectives into the sitting room which had a bay window looking out over the garden. The room was nicely furnished with a comfortable three-piece suite, and a couple of small, highly polished mahogany side tables. The fireplace, which housed an electric coal effect fire, was tiled in a slightly old-fashioned style. She gestured to the detectives to sit. Maguire sat down on the sofa, and Gallagher sat into one of the easy chairs.

"What's this about?" Mrs Hyka said, somewhat brusquely.

"Is Mr Hyka available?" Maguire said

"Yes. I can go and get him, but it would be better if I knew why you are here."

"If you could just go and get him, please, Mrs Hyka, then we will explain fully."

Mrs Hyka left the room, and they could hear her going to the back of the house. She returned a minute later with a very tall, thin man with grey hair dressed in well-cut slacks and a button-down cotton shirt. As they entered the room, Maguire stood up and ushered Mr Hyka back into the hall before he came fully through the door.

Maguire turned the man, and they walked back towards the rear of the house, and went into the kitchen-diner. As they entered the room, the man turned and said in a vexed manner, "What's all this about? Who are you anyway?"

Maguire made sure that they were both out of earshot of the other two, and then she decided to open up.

"We are from the Irish police, Mr Hyka. We are here in connection with your daughter. May I ask you when you last saw, or were in touch with Maria?"

The man looked intensely at Maguire.

"Have you got children?" he said.

"No. I'm not married," Maguire said.

"That isn't always necessary these days," he said, looking away.

"So, when did you last speak to Maria?"

"We don't talk. We are not in touch with her. She has chosen a life that we cannot agree with, so when she left home a few years ago, we said good riddance."

"I see. And what was she doing that you didn't approve of?"

"I don't wish to talk about it. By the way, what is your name?" Hyka asked.

"Oh, sorry, I'm Detective Sergeant Deirdre Maguire, but we are here in an unofficial capacity. I work with the police in Ireland."

"And what has brought you here, Detective Sergeant Maguire?"

"Mr Hyka, there was an incident at a place called Bertra Beach. It's in the west of Ireland, near where I work. A car was burnt out, and when we investigated, we found the body of a young woman in the vehicle. We believe this person was your daughter, Maria."

Hyka looked down at the floor. He didn't say anything for quite some time, and Maguire was wondering what was going through his mind.

Eventually, he looked up, but there were no tears in his eyes. He looked intently at Maguire again, and said, "Perhaps it is just as well. I knew she would come to a bad end."

Chapter Twenty-Eight

In the front room of the Hyka's house, Gallagher got a similar reaction from Maria's mother. She was unemotional, but still took some time to process the news that Gallagher had shared with her. It was obvious that she knew nothing of the incident in advance.

When the conversation went into a lull, Gallagher pressed on.

"Tell me about your son, Mrs Hyka," Gallagher said, looking around at a low table on which several family photographs were arranged in silver frames.

"He's gone too. He left a few years ago, and he doesn't really keep in touch at all."

"Where does he live?"

"He's in London. Oh, he has a good job, and his own place, but he doesn't have much to do with us." The woman looked around to see if her husband was within earshot, and satisfied that he was not, continued, "My husband was very strict with both of them. Especially Marek. He used to beat him quite often if he felt Marek hadn't obeyed him. There was nothing I could do. If I tried to stop him, I would have been hit as well," she said, a little tearfully.

"This must be very difficult for you, Mrs Hyka. I'm sorry," Gallagher said, genuinely feeling for the woman. She thought of all the other women that were in the same position. Essentially enslaved to coercive husbands, but too afraid or unable to do anything about it as they were completely dependent on their men for sustenance.

"Do you have a recent photograph of Marek?"

"Just one he sent me when it was my birthday. He's with his girlfriend."

"May I see it, please?"

Mrs Hyka rummaged in her small handbag and produced a small image of a man with his arms around the shoulder of a pretty young woman.

"May I take a picture of this with my phone?"

"Yes, of course."

Gallagher took out her mobile phone, aimed it at the photograph, and clicked the camera app two or three times.

"Thanks, Mrs Hyka, that's very helpful. And what about Maria? Did she get the same treatment?" Gallagher asked.

"He used to spank her often with a slipper. Right up until the time she left home. It was very undignified. He's put her across his knee with no underwear on her and walloped her five or six times till her skin was red. It was horrible."

"I see. And there was nothing you could have done?"

"What do you think, detective? The only thing I could have done was to leave and take them with me. But I have no money of my own. We would have been on the streets with no roof over our heads and no food; anyway, he is a proud man. He would have come after us, and God knows what would have happened then."

Gallagher felt very sorry for the woman. As her own mother often said to her, 'you never know what goes on behind closed doors', and in this case, it was certainly very true.

Maguire and the father came back into the room, and Gallagher sensed it was time for them to leave. But she wanted to get another piece of information before they left, so she stood up and made sure that Mrs Hyka showed them to the door. On the doorstep, Gallagher asked, "Do you have any contact details for your son, Mrs Hyka. A phone number, or an address, perhaps?"

Once again, Mrs Hyka looked back over her shoulder to see if her husband was observing. When she saw that he wasn't, she made a scribbling gesture with her hand, and Gallagher quickly produced her notebook and a pen. The woman wrote down a phone number in a shaky hand, returned the notebook and pen to Gallagher, and gestured for them to go.

* * *

When they got back in the car, Maguire said nothing at first. She started the engine and drove out of the road where the Hykas lived. They soon encountered a cluster of shops, and Maguire said, "Fancy a coffee?"

"Oh, yes, please. And a bun - I'm famished!"

The small café that was positioned halfway along the small strip of shops was a bit of a mixture. It had all the latest hissing and gurgling coffee machines, and the blackboard at the back of the counter tempted patrons with all the usual varieties of coffee, but the furniture in the place was more of the 1980s. Nevertheless, there was a selection of pastries available, and the two detectives equipped themselves with a large mug of coffee apiece and two enormous fruit scones, accompanied by jam and a little pot of whipped cream each.

When they were seated, Maguire said, "So, what do you make of that then, Agnes?"

Gallagher finished a mouthful of cake, and replied, "It didn't seem like a very happy house, did it? What did the father say?"

"Not much. In fact, very little. I'm not sure if he knows anything, but he was pretty tight-lipped. Did you get anything from the mother?" Maguire said.

"Yes, I did. Seems the father was a very strict disciplinarian. He used to beat both the kids frequently, which is probably why they left as soon as they could. And it looks like they haven't been keeping in touch, which is not surprising. Honestly, some people shouldn't be allowed to have kids."

"I know what you mean. But at least we have a way of following up on the brother now."

Maguire took out her phone and showed Gallagher the picture she had taken of Marek and his girlfriend.

"Hmm. Not a bad-looking chap. Did you get anything else?"

"Yes. A phone number, but no address. I think we'll wait

till we get back home before tackling that though. What do you think?" Maguire said.

"Probably best, unless you fancy a trip to the big smoke. It could be fun. I could do some shopping!"

"That's not what we are here for, Agnes, remember. No. I think we should get back to base. There may be developments that we are unaware of. But it was worth the trip."

* * *

Liam Staunton sat at his desk at the Garda station in Westport. Having left Hanna at the airport, and parted reluctantly from her, he had driven back straight away, unaware that he had been spotted on the road by Maguire and Gallagher.

He was following up as instructed on the phone records from Maria's phone. The printouts had arrived by email from her service provider, and Staunton was going down through them, cross-referencing them to other numbers that they had collected during the investigation.

As he turned over the second page of numbers, he saw something that made his blood run cold. Not quite believing what he was looking at, he reached for his own mobile phone and brought up his own recent call history. Now, there was no doubt. Maria had been in frequent contact with Hanna. There were several calls between them in the days before Maria's death, many of them lasting for several minutes, and one that even went on for over half an hour.

"Shit, shit, shit!" Staunton said out loud, but fortunately, there was no one near enough to hear him. But what should he do now? Maybe his liaison with Hanna wasn't known about - but wait - didn't Maguire know that he had been seeing her?

Chapter Twenty-Nine

DI Martin O'Shea was at work early. He had been told to expect a meeting with Superintendent Derry O'Connell, and he wanted to be as well prepared as possible. When DS Maguire arrived at the Garda station, O'Shea asked her to arrange for a team meeting as soon as everyone had arrived.

"How did you get on in Nottingham, Deirdre?" he said.

"Interesting. We have some good information, but is it OK if I wait till everyone is here to save me from going over it all twice, boss?"

"Yes, of course. Was Agnes helpful?"

"Very."

It wasn't long before Agnes Gallagher and Liam Staunton arrived in too, and Maguire got them all together in the open office. When they were assembled, O'Shea addressed the group.

"Right, everyone. I have a meeting upstairs shortly, so I hope you all have some good news for me. Deirdre, will you go first, please? Tell us how your trip to Nottingham went."

Maguire relayed all the information they had gathered from the Hykas, including the reasons Mrs Hyka had given for the children leaving home. O'Shea was curious.

"Did you follow up on the phone number for the son, or make any attempt to talk to the UK police about it?"

"No, boss. We thought it best to wait till we were back here. I have no idea how to open things up with the London Metropolitan Police, and they could get very annoyed that we had been there at all making enquiries," Maguire said.

"OK. Point taken. I'll see if the super has any ideas. But Marek is obviously a person of interest at this stage, however unlikely it may seem. While we're waiting for all that to develop, why don't you take the photo out to that dodgy car dealer and see if he recognises the lad?"

"Yes, OK, boss. Good idea," Maguire said.

"Liam, how did you get on with the phone records? Anything back yet?" O'Shea said.

"Yes, boss. I have a printout of Maria's calls now. I'm just starting to go through them," Staunton said, not wanting to give details for the moment.

"OK, well, get on with it. There may well be something buried in there that could be significant. Deirdre, will you give Liam Marek's phone number so he can see if Maria was in touch with him at all recently."

"Yes, of course, sir."

"OK. Well, lots to be getting on with. We'll talk again this afternoon before we go home."

The others all agreed in unison, and they dispersed to go back to their own workstations. As Maguire sat down at her desk, Staunton approached.

"Sarge. Can I have a word?" he said.

"Sure, what's on your mind, Liam?"

"Eh, could we go outside for a minute? It's a bit delicate."

Maguire rose from her chair without saying anything, and the two of them went outside to the car park where thankfully, it wasn't raining.

"OK, Liam. What gives?"

"I think I may have been a bit foolish, boss," Staunton said.

"Go on."

"Well, you see, it's Hanna. She needed to get to the airport the other day for a very early flight, so I offered to drive her."

"And?"

"It's a bit embarrassing, boss. I stayed with her the night before. Just because we had to leave in the very small hours to get to Dublin in time, I know it was daft, but, well, you know ..."

"No, Liam, I don't know. I thought we had agreed you wouldn't see her again. This could be very damaging. And by the way, you were seen," Maguire said.

"What! By who?"

"By Agnes Gallagher and me. We spotted you coming back to Westport on the road when we were driving to the airport."

Staunton stayed quiet for a moment or two, but then went on, "And I'm afraid there's more, boss."

"Jesus! What now?"

"I've been looking at Maria Hyka's phone log. She was in regular contact with Hanna in the weeks before she died. Some conversations were quite lengthy, too."

"Bloody hell, Liam. This is dreadful. You know I'll have to tell the boss. You could easily get suspended."

"Aw, shit, boss. Are you serious?"

"Yes. Very. What do you know of this Hanna woman anyway?" Maguire said.

"She comes from somewhere near the Czechia border. She has a son and a mother that she provides for. That's why she comes to Ireland to work as an escort. She said that a couple of weeks doing that would give her enough to support them for three months. I think she's genuine, boss. What happens now?"

"Say nothing till I figure out a way to broach the subject with the DI. I might be able to figure something out, but then again, I might not. Keep your head down, and finish the work analysing the phone records. I want to know if the brother was in touch with Maria recently."

"OK, boss, and thanks."

"Don't thank me yet, Liam. This isn't over."

Chapter Thirty

When Maguire got back to her desk, there was a note stuck to her PC screen asking her to call forensics. She lifted her phone and made the call.

"Hi. Can I speak to Kevin, please?" Maguire said.

"Yes, sure. Hold on a second," the woman said. Maguire waited patiently, trying to process what Liam Staunton had told her, and how she might bring his news to the attention of O'Shea without causing too much damage. After a few moments her thoughts were interrupted by Kevin.

"Hi, Deirdre. It's Kevin. Thanks for calling back. Look, I'm afraid there has been a bit of a cock-up here. You remember that small sticking plaster we recovered from the car where the burnt body of the girl was found out at Bertra?"

"Yes, of course. It had DNA on it that was a familial match to the victim. I think you said that it was probably a sibling. So what?"

"Well, the sample got contaminated with the sample

from the woman herself. I've had the tests re-run, and there's no connection between it and the victim. None at all."

"Jesus, Kevin. How the hell did that happen?" Maguire said. She was livid.

"It's just that we have a few new people here just now that haven't a lot of experience, and the sticking plaster was so small. They just got a bit mixed up. I'm sorry."

"Bloody hell, Kevin, so am I. That's a whole trail of evidence we were following up in smoke, if you'll excuse the pun. Are you sure about this? You won't be calling back in another hour to say that the mistake was a mistake, will you?"

"No, sorry, Deirdre. I supervised the second test personally. I'm quite sure."

"Very well. Thanks for letting me know in any case. I'll catch you later," Maguire said.

"Yes, bye."

When she had finished the call, Maguire went in search of the DI to break the bad news to him, but he had apparently gone upstairs to have his meeting with the superintendent. She didn't know whether or not to interrupt him. He was probably telling O'Connell about the connection between Maria and her brother, which he would have to retract later, making the whole team look a bit inept, even though it wasn't their fault. She was wondering what to do, when Agnes Gallagher approached.

"Got a minute, Sarge?"

"Yes, sure. What's on your mind?"

"Did Liam tell you anything about his early morning adventures on the M6?" Gallagher said.

"Yes, he did," and she went on to tell her colleague what Staunton had said about leaving Hanna at the airport for a flight to Czechia.

"I'm really not looking forward to telling the DI. But I'll have to. And there's more bad news, I'm afraid. The lab got the DNA samples from the car mixed up. There's now no evidence that Maria's brother was here at all. It's all coming undone, Agnes. Listen, can you call Marek's phone and see if you can establish where he was at the time Maria was killed? You'll have to be a bit careful with your questioning, and of course, he may not even know she's dead. Can you handle it, OK?"

"Yes, I think so. I'll give it a go anyway."

* * *

Liam Staunton was keen to get out of the station for a while, so he did as he had been instructed and drove out to Kenny's Karz armed with the photograph of Marek Hyka. He felt there was some chance he could redeem himself if Kenny identified Marek from the picture Maguire and Gallagher had brought back from England.

It was a warm day, with patchy, fluffy clouds slowly drifting across the sky overhead, as Staunton drove out towards Cloona. As he went along, he contemplated his position. He knew he had been stupid to get entangled with Hanna, but she was so totally gorgeous, no one could blame him. He thought of her now, probably back in Czechia with her son and her mother telling them of her adventures in Ireland, and all the money she had earned. He knew it was a rather seedy way of getting cash together for her, but he had a sneaky admiration for her as well, putting her body literally on the line to support her family. He wondered if Hanna would return to Ireland again, and if so, would he get to meet up with her.

He arrived at Kenny's so-called premises, and pulled his car up on the grass alongside Kenny's stock of old bangers. The man himself was standing in front of a silver Volkswagen Passat, which was sixteen years old, and looked quite the worse for wear. He was discussing the vehicle with another, shorter man, whom Staunton assumed to be a customer. Staunton stayed in his car, observing the haggling going on between the two men. After a short while, they shook hands, and the buyer took out a roll of notes, peeling off several and handing them to Kenny. Kenny counted them and stuffed them into his jeans pocket, handing a single key to the purchaser, who sat into the old VW and started the engine. A cloud of dirty black diesel smoke came out of the exhaust pipe, and Staunton could hear the rattle of the engine as it was gently revved. The man did a five-point turn on the narrow road, and eventually drove off back the way Staunton had come in a cloud of more sooty fumes.

Staunton got out of his car and called to the car dealer.

"Mr Kenny. May I have a word, please?"

Kenny turned to look at Staunton, and said, "Yes, of course, are you here to buy a car?"

"No, thanks. I'm Detective Garda Staunton from Westport. I think my colleagues spoke to you before about that Avensis that you sold that ended up burnt out at Bertra beach."

"Oh, yes, I remember. What do you want?" Kenny said,

his interest clearly waning now that he had established that Staunton wasn't a potential customer.

"Could I ask you to have a look at this photograph, and see if you recognize it? It might be the person that purchased the Avensis."

"Give it here, then," Kenny said.

Kenny took the photograph in his grubby hands and studied it.

"Nope. That's not him. Definitely not," he said, offering it back to the young Garda.

"Are you sure, Mr Kenny? Have another look."

"I told you, it's not him. The fella that bought the Avensis was a bit older, and looked completely different. I never forget a face." He thrust the photo back into Staunton's hands.

Staunton just shrugged, put the image back in his pocket, and turned towards his vehicle.

"OK. Well, thanks for trying anyway. I'll leave you to it."

Chapter Thirty-One

It was early afternoon. Agnes Gallagher came across to where Deirdre Maguire was seated at her desk. She waited a moment until Maguire looked up, and then Gallagher said, "Sarge, I've been doing a bit of a nosey into that girl Hanna that Liam has been helping out."

"Oh. Anything of interest?" Maguire said.

"Well, yes, actually. I don't believe she went back to Prague after Liam dropped her off. I checked with the airlines. She was booked to Bristol on the first flight out. She had no onward reservation, and there isn't a flight from Bristol to Prague in any case."

"Are you serious, Agnes? For God's sake! What's going on with this wretched case? Are you quite sure about this?"

"Yes, I'm sure. Ryanair confirmed it. And she came in from Bristol about three weeks previously, too. I think she's living there."

"Do we have Hanna's surname?" Maguire said.

"Yes, the airline confirmed it. It's Babinec. She's Hanna Babinec."

"Right. Well, can you do whatever you can to locate her in the Bristol area using all the usual searches? If it comes to it, contact Bristol police, but try not to give them any details. Just say we need to speak to her. OK? Oh, and Agnes, did you manage to call the brother's number yet?"

"No, sorry, boss. I was too busy with the Hanna thing. I'll get onto it right away."

"No. It's OK. I'll call the brother. You focus on this Hanna creature."

"OK. Thanks, Sarge."

* * *

Maguire would have liked to speak to DI O'Shea straight away to give him all the latest from the case, but he still wasn't around. Instead, she took out the phone number for Marek Hyka, and dialled. The phone was answered on the second ring.

"Hello," a man's voice said.

"Hello. Is that Marek Hyka?" Maguire said.

"Yes. This is Marek. Who's calling, please?"

"My name is Detective Sergeant Maguire, from the Irish police. Have you a few minutes to talk, Mr Hyka?"

"Yes, of course. Is this about my sister Maria?" Hyka said.

"Yes, that's right. What have you heard?"

"I know that she is dead." Hyka paused the conversation at this point, seemingly overcome with grief. Maguire stayed quiet whilst he composed himself. Then he continued.

"Have you discovered what happened, Sergeant?"

"We are actively investigating, Marek. May I ask when you last saw Maria?"

"Let's see. It was about three months ago. We met up in London. Look, I know what she was doing, and you should know that I didn't approve of the way in which she was making a living, but that was her business, not mine. She was still my sister, and I loved her."

"Marek, have you ever been to Ireland?" Maguire said.

"No, not yet. I was hoping to come over this year, but I am very busy here at work, and I couldn't arrange it. Maria said it is a very beautiful country."

"What do you work at, Marek?"

"I work in banking here in the city. I administer hedge funds for them. It's mostly paperwork, but I enjoy it."

"Marek, when were you last in touch with your sister?"

"I telephoned her about ten days ago. She said she had a nice apartment in Westport, and that she would be staying for a few weeks."

"Do you know where she was living in England, Marek?"

"No. Not exactly. But I think it was London. She moved around a lot. We just kept in touch by phone."

"OK. Thanks, Marek, and I'm very sorry about Maria. Before you go, did you ever hear her speaking about a friend called Hanna?"

"Yes, I think so. She told me she had a friend called Hanna who was also in Ireland, but I don't know anything more about this woman."

"OK. Well, thanks for speaking to me, Marek. I know this must be very difficult for you. Do you mind if I call you again if anything crops up?" Maguire said.

"No. Of course not. But please find out who did this terrible thing to my sister, Sergeant."

"I hope we will, Marek. I really do. Goodbye for now."

* * *

O'Shea was back in his office and he called Maguire in.

"Hi, Deirdre. Have we managed to locate the brother of the dead girl yet?"

"Yes, boss. I've just been speaking to him on the phone. But it's not him," Maguire said.

"How do you mean?"

Maguire went on to explain the mix-up at forensics over the DNA sample. She relayed the gist of her conversation with Marek Hyka too, with O'Shea's face getting longer and longer as she spoke.

"Bloody hell, Deirdre. This is a right mess. Have we anything positive to report at all? I've told O'Connell all about the brother now too, and he's under the illusion that we have our man - well at least that we know who he is. I'm not looking forward to giving him this news. He'll go spare."

"I know, boss. We're more or less back to square one. But I have some other news, too."

Maguire went on to explain as tactfully as she could about Liam Staunton's involvement with Hanna Babinec, and the fact that she had returned to the Bristol area of the UK and not Prague, as she had told Staunton.

O'Shea was pensive, and then said, "Maybe that's not all that bad. We might still be able to use it. Are we trying to track this Babinec woman down in Bristol?"

"Yes, of course."

"Well, let me know if we get a fix on her, and don't tell Liam."

"OK, boss. What have you got in mind?"

"I'll tell you if we manage to locate her. Meanwhile, mums the word. We'll have a briefing with the team before we go home. We'll have to make some progress on this thing soon."

"Yes, boss. I hear you," Maguire said, and she left the room.

Chapter Thirty-Two

The day passed slowly. The detectives were busy trying to make sense of the case, and searching various websites to see if they could get any more information on any of the people in Maria Hyka's circle.

At around half past three, Maguire's desk phone rang.

"DS Maguire," she said as she picked up the receiver.

"Oh, good afternoon. My name is Rory McAllister. I have a mobile home out here at Bertra Beach. I've been away for a few weeks, but I'm back here now."

"Very well, Mr McAllister. How can I help you?"

"Well, I believe there was an incident out here a while back when I was away. Is that right?"

"Yes, that's correct. A car was set on fire and when we got to it the body of a young woman was discovered inside it. I'm afraid she was deceased. May I ask what you know of this?" Maguire said.

"Personally, I know nothing at all about it. But I have a camera here rigged up that looks out the front window of my mobile home out across the beach. It's set to record the sunsets in the late evening and the early dawn. I've been watching the footage, and it looks like it recorded the whole thing. Quite a burn up, it was."

"Wow. That could be very helpful, Mr McAllister. Could you make sure that the recording is secure? I'll send someone out to you right away to collect it. Which mobile home are you in?"

"It's the fourth one in from the entrance on the left, overlooking the beach."

"Right, thanks. On second thoughts, I think I'll come out myself and collect it. I should be there in under half an hour."

"OK. Fine. I'll wait here for you."

"Thanks. See you soon."

When the call was ended, Maguire went to find DI O'Shea. She found him in his office working on some reports.

"Boss, I've just had a call from a Rory McAllister out at Bertra Beach. He says he has a video recording of the night the car was burnt out there. I'm going to go out and collect it right away. Do you want to come?"

"I'd love to, but I have to get this finished for the boss. You go ahead. Take one of the others with you if you like. Oh, and see what you think of this McAllister bloke."

"Right, boss. See you later then."

* * *

Maguire collected Agnes Gallagher before setting off to the caravan park. On the drive out to Bertra, she briefed the junior officer.

"Agnes, when we get here, I'll keep McAllister talking. You see, you can have a bit of a look around his gaff. I'm not sure what we're looking for, but the boss wants us to find out as much as we can about this guy."

"Right, Sarge. But it's a mobile home, right? Not much room to hide anything interesting," Gallagher said.

"Just keep your wits about you, Agnes. That's all I'm saying."

The two continued in silence for the rest of the journey, which took them barely twenty minutes. When the road met the Atlantic seaboard, the sun was shining, and the deep aquamarine blue of the ocean with small white caps on the tips of the waves looked magnificent in the late afternoon light.

Maguire pulled her car in through the gates of the caravan park, and drove over the grass until she was in front of the fourth mobile home. The two Gardaí got out and approached the door of the unit, with Maguire stepping up and knocking gently on the glass door. After a moment, the door swung outwards, and Maguire had to step back quickly to avoid being knocked over.

Rory McAllister was a tall, slim man in his mid-forties. He was dressed in blue jeans, and a check cowboy shirt with the sleeves rolled up to his elbows. The man had a rugged appearance and a tanned complexion, as if he worked outdoors in the summer sun.

"Ah, you must be Sergeant Maguire. I'm Rory McAllister," the man said, extending his hand.

"Please, come in, come in."

Maguire ushered Gallagher into the mobile home in front of her while making the introduction.

The front of the unit had a large picture window looking out over the beach at Bertra. It was positioned above the car park so that a panoramic view of the coast and the viewing point where tourists stopped to admire the view could be afforded. Under the window, and extending back on both sides into the floor space, there was a bench seat, and McAllister gestured to the two detectives to sit down. Maguire took her seat, but Gallagher remained standing and retreated slightly backwards into the body of the mobile home.

McAllister remained standing too, and pointed to the small black camera that was mounted at the top of the window, secured to the overhead shelf with a metal bracket.

"This is the camera I was telling you about, Sergeant Maguire. I have it set up to record every evening and every morning. I get some really spectacular sunsets on it. It's triggered by the light, so possibly the headlights of the car, or maybe even the blaze set it running."

"Have you got the recording, Mr McAllister?" Maguire asked.

"Yes. I copied it down onto a little memory card for you. It's all there," he said, picking up an SD card from the shelf behind him and handing it to Maguire.

"Thanks. May I ask what you do for a living, Mr McAllister?"

"I work in Sligo in one of the big healthcare companies there. I'm in I.T. I've been there four years now. It's grand, and I was lucky to have managed to get this thing from my brother, who has moved away to England."

"May I ask if you are married, Mr McAllister?" Maguire said.

"Oh, yes. We have two children, Séan, who is four years old, and Niamh. She's six, going on twenty!" he said, smiling broadly.

"And how often do you get down here?" Maguire said.

"Most weekends in the summer. The kids love the beach, and it's nice to get away from work for a couple of days and chill out."

"And what brought you down here today?" Maguire said.

"I've been away on business for a couple of weeks, and I don't like to leave the place unattended for too long. Besides, we needed a new gas bottle. So, I took an hour off and came down to check it out."

"I see. I'm glad you did. This could be very useful to us," Maguire said, holding up the little memory card.

McAllister smiled.

"What went down anyway? McGroarty told me someone had died."

"Yes, I'm afraid so. We are investigating the whole business right now. I'm afraid I can't say much about it. Do you have a lot of dealings with Mr McGroarty?"

"Not a whole lot. I pay him the site fees, of course, and occasionally there are some other matters we have to discuss about the services on the site. But I usually only see him once or twice a season. Sorry. Would you ladies like a cup of tea or coffee?"

"No thanks, we're fine. In fact, we'd better be getting back. Could I ask you to jot down your contact details in my notebook in case we need to speak to you again?"

"Yes, of course. Give it here."

McAllister sat on the edge of the seat as he wrote his

details into Maguire's pocket book. When he had finished, he returned it to her, and she stood up, preparing to go.

"Come along, Agnes. We need to get back to Westport."

Maguire said goodbye to Rory McAllister, and the two of them got back into Maguire's car and left.

Chapter Thirty-Three

Back at the Garda station, Maguire found Liam Staunton sitting at his desk. She approached him, holding up the little blue SD card like a trophy.

"Liam. I have a present for you. This little number may have a recording of the person who set the fire out at Bertra. We need to be very careful with it. Can you start by making a copy of the entire content, see if you can find the important bits, then give me a shout," Maguire said.

"Yes, sure, Sarge. How did you manage to get hold of that?"

"The lovely Rory McAllister gave me a present of it. And while you're at it, see if we have anything on him too. He works in one of the pharma outfits near Sligo, and I have his home address if you need it."

"OK. I'll come and find you if I get anything."

"Thanks," Maguire said. She then went off to find DI O'Shea to bring him up to speed.

She found O'Shea still in his office.

"Sorry to disturb you again, boss, but we've had a

development," Maguire said. She went on to explain about the visit to the caravan site, and the little gem that McAllister had given them.

"Liam is just exploring it now. With a bit of luck, we might get a look at the driver of the car."

"Hmph .. don't hold your breath. The way things are going, it will probably be blank!"

"Don't be such a pessimist, boss. Something has to give sooner or later. And I have Agnes trying to track down Hanna Babinec, too. Apparently, she lives in the Bristol area somewhere, and with a name like that, she can't be that difficult to find."

"OK. Well, let's see what we have at five-thirty. Now, can I have a bit of peace to finish this blasted report?"

"Yes, sorry, boss. I'll close the door."

* * *

O'Shea brought everyone together at the end of the working day. He stood at the front of the little group, close to the whiteboard that bore a picture of Maria Hyka, the beach, the McGroartys, and Hanna Babinec.

"OK, everyone. Settle down. Liam, have you had a good look at that footage Sergeant Maguire brought back from the caravan park?" O'Shea said.

"Yes, sir. McAllister was right. The lights of the Avensis did trigger the camera to start recording. The time stamp indicates 3:25am, and you can see the car arriving and parking facing out to sea. The camera keeps recording, and you can see the driver get out a few minutes later. He then disappears for about seven minutes, comes back with a can, and pours the contents over and into the car before lighting a rag and throwing it in, too. Then the whole thing goes up, and yer man runs off," Staunton says.

"Can you get a good look at the arsonist?" Maguire said.

"No, Sarge. But I think the tech boys up in Dublin might be able to clean up the image. He hasn't got a mask on or anything."

"OK. Well, when we're done here, I want us all to look at that video and see if we can spot anything. Sorry, boss, what were you saying?" Maguire said.

"Thanks, Deirdre. Yes, now what about you, Agnes? Have you had any luck locating Hanna Babinec in Bristol?" O'Shea said.

Liam Staunton put up his hand.

"Yes, Liam. What is it?" O'Shea said.

"I think Hanna is in Prague, sir, not Bristol. She lives in Prague with her son and her mother."

"I'm afraid not, Liam. When you dropped her off at Dublin airport, she got on a flight to Bristol, and there's no onward service to Prague. Agnes, have you tracked her down?"

"Not yet, sir. But I've been on to Social Services over there. They were very helpful. I have the name of a woman who is trawling through their records for me. She said she'd call me back tomorrow morning," Gallagher said.

"Good idea. She must be in the system one way or another. I'll talk to you later about all of that, Liam," O'Shea said.

Staunton had gone bright red about the face. He wasn't looking forward to whatever O'Shea might have to say to him.

"Have we anything else then?" O'Shea said, but his question was met with silence.

"OK. Let's go and have a look at some horror video, then. Liam, can you send the clip to the big screen?"

"Yes, sure, boss."

They all stood up and gathered around the large 60-inch TV that was mounted on the wall between the two windows of the open plan. After a bit of fiddling around, the screen came to life with slightly blurred images of the beach at Bertra. They watched as the old Avensis pulled into the car park, and as Staunton had said, the driver got out, disappeared for a few minutes, and then returned to set the fire.

Maguire was the first to speak.

"Anyone spots anything?" she said.

Agnes Gallagher responded.

"Where did he get the petrol, Sarge? It wasn't in the boot of the car. He must either have known where to find it or planted it there in advance."

"That's just what I was thinking, Agnes. Good spot. It must have taken him about three minutes to go to wherever it was stored and another three to bring it back. We need to get out there again and see what is within that distance from where the car was burnt out and where petrol can be stored. I don't remember seeing anything like that when we were out there, but we could easily have missed it. Boss, can you and I go out there tomorrow morning and have a look around?" Maguire said.

"Yes, good idea. Let's go early. We can meet here at nine and set off then. Right, let's leave it for tonight. We all have lots to do tomorrow. Off you go." O'Shea said.

On the way to her car, Maguire called Eoin McNally.

"Hi, Eoin. Are you free this evening? I could do with some company."

"Yes, I was thinking the same. Shall I call for you at about seven, and we can get some grub?"

"Yes, I'd love that. See you soon."

Chapter Thirty-Four

Eoin McNally arrived at Maguire's place at the appointed hour, on time as usual. Maguire had showered, washed her hair, applied her make up, and was looking very smart in a pair of white tailored jeans and a pink top. She threw a matching lightweight pink cardigan over her shoulders, and opened the door.

"Wow! You look amazing," McNally said, advancing on Maguire and giving her a brief kiss.

"Thank you, kind sir. And where are you taking your amazing-looking girlfriend this evening, pray tell?" she responded, smiling broadly.

"What about a picnic out at Bertra Beach, Sergeant?"

"Not funny, Eoin. Not funny at all!" Maguire said, scowling.

"Sorry! I've booked a place in town. It's new, but I've heard good reports. Shall we?"

"Great. Let's go!"

* * *

The Harbour Court restaurant was in its third iteration as a hostelry. Unhappily, the previous sets of owners had failed to make it viable, and it had suffered bankruptcy twice over. But the new owners had invested heavily in the premises, bringing it right up to date with new decor, new furniture, and fully refurbished kitchens.

The menu was largely seafood, which both of them enjoyed, and the service was prompt and attentive without being obtrusive. Although the prices were a bit more than Maguire was used to, the variety on the menu, and the fact that the place was quite full, set her mind at ease.

When they were seated and had ordered their meal, McNally poured Maguire a generous glass of Chardonnay, giving himself a much smaller helping. He raised his glass and said, "To us, Deirdre," and Maguire reciprocated.

As the meal progressed, McNally brought the conversation around to the mysterious case that Maguire was working on.

"Any progress with that business out at Bertra?"

"Not a lot. We have secured some video evidence now of the night the car was set on fire, but I'm not sure that it will get us much further. We have had to send it to Dublin to see if they can enhance it a bit. It's quite blurred, but I think it's all there. We can see the person that set the fire pouring what I presume is petrol into the car and lighting it," Maguire said.

"Cool. That would be great if you could get an I.D. I was thinking about you and your puzzle earlier today at work, and I did a bit of digging on the McGroartys. It turns out they have quite a property portfolio."

"Oh. Really. What does it amount to?"

"Well, they have the caravan site, obviously, and the two apartments on Tober Hill. But McGroarty also has a few places in town. They're not up to a whole lot, but I'm sure they bring in a good bit of rent in the summer months. We have the insurance on them all."

"Can you remember where they are located, Eoin?"

"I think so. He has a couple of places on High Street. I think they are set in flats or apartments as he would have it. And there's one on Mill Street too. Then I think he has a couple of shops that are rented out on long leases in the centre. Why? Is this important?"

"Could be. Listen, I'm sorry to ask, but could you get me a list of all the properties you insure for him and email it to me tomorrow?"

"I guess so. I don't think that's breaking any laws. Am I officially helping the Gardaí with their enquiries?" McNally said with a cheeky grin.

"Definitely. And if you don't co-operate, I have a pair of handcuffs ready back at mine!"

"Hmm .. interesting, Sergeant. Let's finish our food and get out of here, and I promise not to co-operate at all, so you can have your wicked way with me. Are you into police brutality?"

"You'll see," Maguire said, smiling broadly.

* * *

When they left the restaurant, having been very well fed, albeit at a price, they drove back to Maguire's place, and Eoin went in with her. Far from any rough stuff, the two of them enjoyed a warm, intimate, and gentle night together, making love more than once. They eventually fell asleep in the small hours of the morning, and slept soundly till Maguire's alarm clock woke them with a start at 7am.

"Hey, sleepy head. We need to get up," she said, silencing the annoying buzzer that had broken their slumber.

McNally rolled over in the bed, and said, "God! It can't be that time already. I need more sleep."

"Tough! I'm first in the shower, then I'll cook breakfast while you're doing your ablutions. C'mon. Get a move on!"

"This is police brutality," McNally said as he reached out to grab Maguire, but she was too quick for him. She had escaped to the bathroom already.

Chapter Thirty-Five

As Liam Staunton arrived at the station the following morning, Maguire intercepted him on his way to his desk.

"Liam, just a sec."

"Hi, Sarge, what's up?" he said, removing his outer jacket and placing it on the back of his chair.

"You know when you were out checking on the call girls here in the town. Did you keep a note of the addresses?" Maguire said.

"Yes, of course. There was one on High Street, and the other one was on Mill Street, but I have the actual addresses in my pocket book. Do you want them?"

"Yes, please. And then I need to have a word."

Staunton was apprehensive about what was to come. He knew he had been foolish in his actions with Hanna Babinec, and he didn't know how all that was going to work out. He sure as hell didn't want a disciplinary on his record. That could block any hopes of promotion he harboured for the foreseeable future. He went and retrieved his pocket book from his jacket and opened it on the page with the addresses, and gave it to Maguire.

"There you go."

"Thanks. Now grab a seat for a minute while I copy these down."

Staunton did as he was told. When Maguire had finished writing down the details, she turned to Staunton.

"OK, Liam. As you know, Hanna Babinec is living in Bristol. She does have a son, but no sign of her mother. She's been drawing unemployment benefit and child benefit as well as single parent's allowance for a few years now, and she has applied for leave to remain as an EU citizen following Brexit. That application is still being processed."

"Crickey. I really thought she was living in Prague. She had me properly fooled."

"Yes, I know. But listen, we may be able to use this to our advantage. I've been talking to the DI, and he wants to see if we could get her to come back here. She's somehow involved in this Maria Hyka thing, and we have no hope of pursuing it if she's in the UK. The local police won't be interested, and we have no jurisdiction there, of course. So, do you think you could persuade her to come over to Ireland for a dirty weekend?"

"Bloody hell, Sarge! That's a big ask."

"It is, but it would help your case a lot, and no one wants to see you getting a black mark for what you did, which was obviously way out of order," Maguire said.

Staunton remained silent for a few moments, contemplating the situation. Then he looked Maguire in the eye.

"I could give it a try, I guess. I'd probably have to pay

her air fare, and I'd have to keep up the pretence that she is living in Prague, so it might not be cheap. What will happen to her when she gets here?"

"We'll interview her. Technically, she has lied to the police, and she may be guilty of obstruction too, or possibly perverting the course of justice. But I actually think there's a bit more to it. There's something going on with all these call girls, and I think it may have gotten Maria Hyka killed. We know Hanna was in touch with Maria quite often, and we need to get to the bottom of it. It's time for you to decide if your career in the force is more important than your feelings for Hanna, Liam."

Staunton blushed visibly.

"Well, that's a no-brainer, Sarge. Of course, my career is more important to me. And the way Hanna has been behaving doesn't exactly signal the prospect of a long and stable relationship, not to mention her line of work. No, have no fear; I'm a cop first and always."

"That's good to hear, Liam. I'm glad you're being sensible. So, why don't I leave it to you to figure out the details, and then you can come and tell me if you have it all set up, and hopefully, when Hanna Babinec is arriving back. She'll come to Dublin obviously, and we can arrange a welcoming committee for her and get her driven here. I suggest you stay out of it after that till we have some kind of outcome."

"Yes, OK, Sarge. Is that all?"

"Yes, for now at least. Chat to you later."

Staunton got up and went to sit at his own desk. Maguire turned to her own desk and noticed that Eoin McNally had sent her an email. She opened the file.

The email contained a list of all the properties that Mr Gerald Francis McGroarty owned in the Westport area. The two properties that Liam Staunton had written down in his notebook were there, as well as the caravan site and the house on Tober Hill of course, but there were two other properties listed in the centre of town as well.

Maguire acknowledged the email back to Eoin, and said to herself, *"now, aren't you the little treasure, Mr McNally."*

She sent the email to the printer, and collected the page with the addresses on it. She then went across to where Liam Staunton was sitting, contemplating his future.

"Liam, I have a list of properties owned by Gerry McGroarty here. We know about most of them, but there are two we hadn't encountered previously. Could you go out and see if they are occupied, and if so, by whom. Don't be too gentle. Take Agnes with you if you like."

Staunton wasn't sure why Maguire had suggested that Gallagher should accompany him. Was she concerned that he might get led astray again? Or was she just making sure that the occupants of McGroarty's properties would be sufficiently intimidated by the presence of two Gardaí to take them seriously? He didn't know, but he would do as Maguire had suggested in any case.

Chapter Thirty-Six

The first property that Staunton and Gallagher called to was one that the Gardaí had been unaware of until Eoin McNally had sent his list to Maguire. It was on St Mary's Crescent where an enormously long terrace of modest houses looked out onto a huge green space. The houses were all very well-tended with neat, if small, front gardens and fresh paintwork. Number 34 fitted the pattern, and the two detectives opened the little wrought iron gate and approached the front door.

The door jamb had an intercom fitted to it, thankfully without a camera. Staunton pressed the button that was illuminated by a feint blue light. After a moment, a woman's voice answered.

"Yes. Who is this, please?" she said in a distinctly foreign accent.

"My name is Raymond," Staunton lied.

"Have you an appointment, Raymond?"

"No. I'm sorry. A friend told me about this place. Are you available now for half an hour?"

"Just a minute."

Staunton could hear a whispered conversation taking place between two women, and then the one who had answered the doorbell was back.

"Yes, OK. But it will be eighty euro. Is that OK?"

"Yes, of course," Staunton said, looking at Gallagher and rolling his eyes to heaven.

The release on the door buzzed and Staunton and Gallagher entered the house with their warrant cards at the ready.

Inside the house, the two women that they had heard having a whispered conversation were both standing in the hallway. They were probably in their late twenties, dressed in rather provocative clothing, but both very pretty with terrific figures and a healthy sun tan. The woman who was standing behind went for her mobile phone.

"Put that down, NOW!" Gallagher roared at her, which caused her to drop the device on the floor with a loud clatter.

"Let's go in here, and we can have a chat ladies." Staunton said, indicating the room at the front of the house. The two women went into the little room, which was very clean but rather sparsely furnished. There was a sofa though, and they both sat down.

"Are you arresting us?" the first woman said.

"That depends. Let's start with your names," Gallagher said, perching on the arms of the sofa.

The two women looked at each other, and then the one who had opened the door said, "Monika, with a 'k'. And this is Svetlana," she said, gesturing to her companion.

And where are you from, Monika?" Gallagher said.

"We are both from Czechia, near to Prague."

"OK, thanks. I'll need to see your passports in a minute to check your details. What are you doing here?" Gallagher went on.

"Working."

"Working at what?" Gallagher said.

"Isn't it obvious? But it's not illegal. We only charge for our time, not sex," Monika said.

"OK. Who brought you here, Monika?" Staunton asked.

"We can't say. It would not be safe. We would be hurt, or maybe killed if we say anything, like that girl at the seaside."

"Did you know her?" Gallagher said.

"We know about her, that's all," Svetlana replied.

"How do you get your clients?" Staunton said.

"We have a website. We are only here for a few weeks, then we move on," Monika said.

"Do you know a woman by the name of Maria Hyka?" Gallagher asked.

The women looked at each other before Monika replied, "No, I don't know that name."

"What about Hanna Babinec?" Staunton said.

The two of them shook their heads.

"Who do you pay for your time here?" Gallagher said.

"A man comes and collects the rent every week. He's a big guy. I don't like him. He's rough. But once we give him his money, he leaves us alone, well except for last week."

"What happened last week?" Gallagher said.

"We were a little short with the rent, so he had sex with me instead. It was awful. He wasn't clean," Svetlana said.

Svetlana was the prettiest of the two women. She was blonde, slim, and tall, with good legs and a lovely face.

"Do you have a name for this man?" Staunton said.

"Not a proper name. He told us to call him 'Mac', that's all," Svetlana said.

Monika sniggered.

Staunton looked at her expectantly.

"Yes, but I looked in his wallet while you were busy with him. I saw his identity card. It said Gerry Mac-Orty or something like that. And I took a little of his cash, too. He had hundreds of euro stuffed in there. He won't miss a hundred or so."

Staunton shook his head.

"You shouldn't be telling me about taking his money, Monika. But anyway, we will keep that to ourselves. But listen girls, I think you should pack up here now and move on. Go back to wherever you came from. You may be in danger, and we wouldn't want anything to happen to you. If I were you, I'd pack a bag and vanish."

"Are you not going to arrest us?" Monika said.

"No, we are not. Just leave, and don't come back this way. Do you have any other friends working here just now?"

"No, nobody."

"OK. Then I suggest you leave today. Don't tell anyone where you are going; just go. All right?"

"OK. And thank you," Svetlana said.

"Don't mention it," Staunton said, smiling.

* * *

Gallagher and Staunton called the second new address on the list when they had left Monika and Svetlana, but there was no reply at the door. Staunton figured that the word must have got out amongst the escort community, and they were all doing a runner. He wondered if Hanna was being informed.

Chapter Thirty-Seven

O'Shea and Maguire set off from the Garda station in Westport, heading for the site of the car fire out at Bertra. O'Shea was driving, and was pushing it a bit. Maguire felt slightly uncomfortable with the pace, so she said, "Are we in a hurry, boss?" Maguire said.

"No, sorry. Was I pasting it a bit?" he said, easing off the accelerator a little.

"Just a tad, boss. What have you in mind when we get there?"

"I want us to stand at the spot where the car was burnt and walk briskly for about three minutes away from it, and see where we end up. One of us can go left, and the other right. Then we come back and compare notes."

"OK. What are you hoping to find?" Maguire said.

"I'm not sure. But it looks from the video that McAllister recorded that the arsonist went somewhere to get the fuel. He didn't appear to have it with him, and he was gone for about seven minutes. If we can find where it was stashed, we might be a bit further on."

"Ah, I see what you mean. Good idea."

O'Shea gave his colleague a sideways glance, and after another couple of minutes of silence, he said, "How are things going with Eoin, Deirdre?"

"Pretty good. And he's proving to be pretty useful with this case too. It was he who discovered the other apartments that McGroarty has in the town. They are all insured with his company."

"That's handy, but it's not actually what I meant. I was talking personally," O'Shea said.

"Ah, ye know. We get along great. He's very attentive and quite the gentleman. Maybe a bit too much so. But I'm fond of him all the same," Maguire said.

O'Shea went silent again, processing what she had said, so she went on, "Why do you ask anyway?"

"I'll level with you, Deirdre. As I'm sure you have observed, I'm building quite a team here in Westport. It wasn't really supposed to happen, but then we had that thing involving the farm killings, and we kind of got noticed a bit by the suits. I'm just curious to know if you will be around for a while, that's all."

"Would you like me to be?"

"Yes, definitely," O'Shea said without hesitation. "You're a very good detective. Just what I need as my right-hand man, or should I say person, in these days of political correctness?"

"Woman would be OK too, boss," she said, laughing.

"Well, whatever. And in my own very selfish way, I

thought if you had a romantic involvement with someone local, you'd be more inclined to stay. Am I right?"

"Nope. I don't connect the two things at all. I'll stay because I enjoy working with you, Liam and Agnes. You're right about one thing, though. We do make a formidable team. And if we manage to crack this one, we'll all be up for gold stars."

"If only, Deirdre. If only."

* * *

O'Shea pulled in at the viewing point at Bertra Beach, selecting the nearest space that they encountered. There was no other vehicle in the parking area, and they could both see where the new surface had been put down by the council following the fire. They got out of the car.

"OK. You go off to the right, and I'll go left. Walk briskly for, say, two minutes and see where it takes you. Pause for a couple of minutes and then walk back. I'll do the same in the other direction and then come back here," O'Shea said.

Maguire set off as directed. Her two-minute walk took her to the main entrance to the caravan site, where she spotted a wooden shed just inside the gate, over to the side. She went to the door of the little building, only to find that it was secured with a shiny and substantial padlock. She turned and walked back to where the car had been set on fire, arriving just as O'Shea returned from his short walk.

"Well?" she said.

"Nothing. Just a sandy path down to the sea. What about you?"

"There's a small wooden shed at the entrance to the park. It's just inside the gate on the right. But it's locked. Do you think we should go and talk to McGroarty about it? Maybe get him to open it up."

"No. Obviously, it could have been where the petrol was stored, but I want to set things up a bit more carefully before we go knocking on his door. Let's get back to base and have a chat with the others," O'Shea said.

"OK. You're the boss."

* * *

Back in the Garda station, O'Shea asked Staunton and Gallagher to come into his office. Maguire was already seated in front of his desk. O'Shea addressed the team.

"Right, everyone. The more we dig into this, the more the name McGroarty keeps cropping up. I think the two of them are somehow connected to what's been going on, but they are smart. I don't want to go charging in and accusing them of heaven knows what. We're going to have to outwit them. So, this is what I have in mind."

O'Shea went on to outline his plan, much to the surprise of the rest of the team. When he had finished, he told them all to go home, except for Liam Staunton, who was to remain behind. When it was just O'Shea and Staunton in the room, O'Shea spoke up.

"OK, Liam. Now I've been hearing all about your shenanigans with this Hanna Babinec woman. You know your involvement there is pretty serious. It's against just about every regulation I can think of, and by rights, you should be suspended by now. But I'm not a vindictive man,

Liam, and I think we might just be able to turn this to our advantage and get you off the hook, as it were."

Staunton perked up when he heard this. He was fully expecting to get a right telling off over his involvement with Hanna, or even worse, but now the DI was holding out some hope of a let off. He couldn't help smiling as he said to the senior officer, "What can I do to help, sir?"

"I presume you still have Hanna Babinec's phone number, Liam?"

"Yes, I do. The number is from Czechia, but it seems she's actually in Bristol."

"Yes, that's what I have heard too. But, listen, let's keep up the subterfuge that she's in Czechia. But I want you to call her and persuade her to come back to Ireland for a few days," O'Shea said.

"Yes. Sergeant Maguire said that might be on the cards. I'll certainly give it a try. Any idea what I could use as bait?" Staunton said.

"I dunno. Have a word with Deirdre. She knows how a woman's mind works. Figure something out. To be honest, it might be better if I didn't know."

"Yes, sir, I know what you mean. OK. Leave it with me. I'll let you know if I get her hooked."

"Great. Well, off you go. You might just catch Sergeant Maguire before she disappears."

Chapter Thirty-Eight

Liam Staunton's mind was in turmoil. On the one hand, he knew that he badly needed to redeem himself with Maguire and O'Shea. If he didn't manage to do that, he could find himself in serious trouble. But on the other hand, he had developed a strong affection for Hanna Babinec. The woman had really got under his skin. He knew it was a hopeless situation with her, and maybe that was what was making him all the more anxious to be with her. Forbidden fruit, as it were.

He spent an hour or so thinking about his upcoming phone call, and then went to a quiet area in the station and dialled her number. She answered almost at once.

"Hello, Hanna. It's me, Liam. How are you keeping?"

"Oh, hi, Liam. Nice to hear from you. I'm good, thanks. I'm back in Czechia now with my son and my mother. It's nice to be back home. How are you getting on?"

Staunton swallowed the lie, knowing that Hanna was actually in the United Kingdom. He went on, "Hanna, have you missed me at all?"

"Yes, of course, Liam," Hanna said, lowering her voice and speaking a little closer to the phone.

"I know this is a bit strange, Hanna, but I was wondering if you would come over to visit me for a couple of days? I'd pay your air fare, you could stay with me, and we could go shopping for your son, get him some nice things."

"Gosh, Liam. I'd love to see you, but it could be a little bit tricky for me to get away," Hanna said.

Staunton allowed the disappointment to show in his voice.

"I know, love, but it would mean a lot to me, and I'd make it as easy as possible for you. I'll collect you at Dublin airport, and leave you back, and it won't cost you a penny. What do you say?"

Hanna remained silent for a moment, then said, "Can you leave me to decide for a while, Liam? I'd love to see you, but I'm not sure. Call me again tomorrow. I'll tell you then."

"OK, love. Thanks," Staunton said.

He didn't feel good about deceiving the woman in this way, but he rationalized it by reminding himself that Hanna had lied to him about where she was living, and probably a lot more besides. But he still felt a bit uneasy about the subterfuge.

When he had finished the call, and taken a few minutes to steady himself, he went in search of Maguire to update her.

* * *

DI O'Shea was feeling restless. The case was going too slowly for his liking, and the layers of complexity had the entire team stumped. He went to find DS Maguire.

"Deirdre, got a minute?"

"Yes, sure, boss," she said, looking up from her PC screen.

"Do you know if we have Gerry McGroarty's prints on file?"

"I can check, but I don't think so. Why?"

"Can you retrieve that red plastic petrol can that forensics found at Bertra after the car fire? Leave it in the evidence bag, but come and find me when you have it. OK?"

"Yes, sure," Maguire said. She wasn't at all sure what her boss wanted, but she knew not to challenge him when he was in that mood. She went to the evidence lock-up and found the item that he had requested. She returned to the office, where she found O'Shea pacing the floor.

"Good. Now, I want you and me to go out to the caravan park, and bring your fingerprint kit."

"OK. Give me a minute, and I'll be with you."

When they were in O'Shea's car heading for Bertra Beach, Maguires asked her colleague, "What have you got in mind, boss?"

"We're going to have to play it by ear, Deirdre. I have a feeling that both the McGroartys are somehow connected to this whole business. I just can't slot it into place. What do you think?"

"It seems a bit unlikely to me, boss. OK, so the wife has rented her apartments out to the escort girls. She may or may not have known what they were doing, but it hardly makes her a madam," Maguire said.

"Hmm.. I'm not convinced. Have we had any luck with the video from the mobile home?"

"Not yet. It's still with the techies up in Dublin. I'll follow it up when we get back."

It didn't take them long to get to the caravan site. There were a few hired cars on the route being driven cautiously, so that the occupants, who were obviously tourists, could admire the scenery as they progressed along the road. O'Shea passed most of them when it was safe to do so, and cursed silently to himself when he had to hang back.

When they got to Bertra, he pulled his car in through the entrance and stopped outside the mobile home that was being used as an office. They both got out, with Maguire taking the red petrol can in the evidence bag off the back seat.

The door of the office was open, being held wide by a brick. Maguire stood on the step and looked in. The office was relatively tidy, but there was no one inside that she could see. She called out a few times but got no response. She turned to O'Shea and said, "There's no one in, boss."

"OK. Well, let's have a look around out here. He can't be far away if the place is open to the four winds. You go straight up the back, and I'll go left here along in front of the units. Give a shout out if you find him."

The two of them went in the agreed directions. O'Shea was first to encounter Gerry McGroarty, who was doing some maintenance work on one of the static caravans. He called to his colleague before engaging the man in conversation.

"Good day, Mr McGroarty," O'Shea said, "hard at it, I see."

McGroarty, who was dressed in a dark blue boiler suit and was holding a heavy adjustable wrench, stood up.

"Ah, sure, you know how it is. Someone has to keep the damn things going. What can I be doing for you today, anyway?"

"We're just following up on enquiries, Mr McGroarty," O'Shea said as Maguire joined him. O'Shea gestured to the bag that Maguire was holding.

"Have you ever seen this item before, Mr McGroarty?"

McGroarty lifted the evidence bag up and looked inside.

"Well, I don't know if it's the same one. But I have one of them myself. It's in the shed down by the gate. I use it for the lawnmower and hedge trimmer."

"I wonder if we could just go and see if it's still there, Mr McGroarty?" O'Shea said.

"Sure, of course, it is. Where else would it be?"

"If we could just check, please, sir."

McGroarty grunted, but he put down his spanner, and walked off a little huffily towards the entrance. O'Shea and Maguire followed behind.

When they got to the store, McGroarty took a set of keys from his pocket and opened the lock on the door, pulling it open. As he did so, a light came on inside. The place was neatly arranged with a bench along one side, above which various tools were hanging on a board. The bench was clean and clutter-free. McGroarty bent down to look underneath, moving a few cardboard boxes around. After a minute or two, he stood up, scratching his head.

"That's a quare one now altogether. It doesn't seem to be where I left it."

"I see," O'Shea said. "Mr McGroarty, I wonder would you mind giving us a set of fingerprints, just for the purpose of elimination? Sergeant Maguire has a little device here that we can use. You don't need to get ink or anything on your hands. It's all electronic these days."

McGroarty thought for a while.

"Ah, I suppose so. How long will it take?"

Maguire stepped forward, taking the fingerprint machine from her jacket pocket.

"Just a couple of minutes, sir. We can do it here on the bench."

They went through the brief procedure, and Maguire thanked the man for his cooperation.

"We'll leave you to it, Mr McGroarty," Maguire said, and the two detectives walked back to O'Shea's car.

Chapter Thirty-Nine

Hanna Babinec was a clever woman. She had managed to get Liam Staunton to part with over €400 for a return flight from Prague to Dublin, and she had booked a flight from Bristol to Dublin that was timed to arrive at the same time as the Prague flight on Saturday morning. The return flight from Bristol to Dublin was only €84, and she was pleased to be able to pocket the difference. Staunton was well aware of the subterfuge, but was happy to go along with it in order to get the woman back to Westport to be properly interviewed.

He met Hanna at Dublin airport when she arrived. They embraced warmly in the arrivals area, and then Staunton offered her some refreshment.

"You must be hungry after your early start. Would you like some breakfast, or maybe a coffee before we set off?" Staunton said.

"No thanks, Liam. Let's just get on the road. We can stop along the way if you like?" she said.

"Yes, OK. My car is out the front here. One of the

privileges of being a Garda, we can park in the set down area," Staunton said smiling.

"Don't be a policeman today, Liam," she said, linking arms with Staunton and towing her wheelie case along with her free hand.

When they got to his car, Staunton loaded Hanna's case into the boot, and then held the passenger's door open for her. They set off for the west.

As they drove along, they chatted about this and that. Staunton was careful not to reveal that he knew Hanna was actually living in the UK. He managed to keep his chatter focused on Czechia.

"What are the winters like where you live, Hanna?"

"Bitter cold, but usually dry, so it's not the same as here where it seems to be always raining."

"Well, that's why Ireland is called the Emerald Isle. All the rain makes the grass green. But we are used to it. It doesn't bother us too much at all really."

The conversation continued in much the same vein as Staunton navigated his way across the country. When they got as far as Athlone, he suggested a pit stop for refreshments, and he pulled into the big service station just off the M6, which catered to all types of food and drink.

When they were indoors, Hanna went off to the bathroom while Staunton collected two coffees and a couple of pastries to sustain them for the rest of the journey. Staunton noticed that the woman had taken her mobile phone with her to the washroom. He was hoping to have a snoop in it while she was gone, but she was too smart for that.

Back on the road, Hanna dozed, leaning against

Staunton's shoulder, and he remained quiet, concentrating on the driving. They were approaching Westport by late morning, and Staunton drove straight to the Garda station.

Hanna awoke from her slumber and saw at once where they were. She wasn't at all happy.

"What's happening, Liam? Why are we here?"

"It's OK. I just have to do a little work inside. You can come in with me if you like and I'll get you a coffee or something while you are waiting."

"How long will you be?" Hanna said.

"Maybe twenty minutes or so. Why don't you come in with me?"

"Yes, OK."

DI O'Shea had primed the desk sergeant to look out for the arrival of Staunton's car, and as soon as he saw it pulling up, he called O'Shea and advised him. O'Shea collected Maguire, and the two of them went downstairs, arriving in the front office just as Staunton and Babinec came in through the door.

O'Shea addressed Babinec.

"Good morning, Ms Babinec. I trust you had a pleasant flight. You must have been up very early. My name is Detective Inspector O'Shea, and this is my colleague, Detective Sergeant Maguire. We need to have a little chat with you. Would you come with us, please?"

Hanna Babinec looked at Staunton with a bewildered expression, but Staunton remained unmoved. He excused himself, and went upstairs.

Babinec was ushered to an interview room where O'Shea and Maguire sat opposite her at the grey-topped table.

"Before we start, Ms Babinec, I want to explain that you

are not under arrest; you are simply helping us with our enquiries. You are free to leave at any time, and if you feel the need, you may have a solicitor present. Is that clear?"

"What is all this about?" she replied. Maguire decided to take up the discussion.

"Hanna, we need to know exactly what is going on with your associates here in Westport. I'm talking about Alena, Maria, and the other girls."

"How should I know? I have already explained to Liam that I work on my own. I come here for two or three weeks every few months to make some money for my son and my mother in Czechia. I don't know about any other girls."

Maguire looked sideways at O'Shea, signalling that he should continue.

"That's not strictly speaking true, Ms Babinec, is it? We know that you are living in Bristol, in England, and you live with just your son. So why have you lied to us?"

"What kind of trick is this?" Babinec said angrily. "I have done nothing wrong, unlike your colleague. Is it a common practice for the police here to go with escort girls and not pay them?" she said, sitting back in her chair and folding her arms in front of her.

O'Shea pressed on.

"Look, Hanna, none of that is relevant. We are trying to solve a murder here. Maria Hyka was brutally killed, and her body was then burned beyond recognition. She was an escort girl too, so you could be in great danger. If you tell us what you know, we can protect you."

"Pah! Do I look like I need your protection?" she said, and looked away.

Maguire picked up the questioning again.

"Hanna, we don't really care what you get up to. We know there are sex workers operating around here, and as long as there's no violence or any risk to ordinary people, we let it go on, because it's easier that way. And if you fed Liam Staunton a sob story and got him to give you some money for a phony airfare, so be it. But when something like what happened to Maria Hyka crops up, we have to deal with it. I'm sure you understand. Now, have you any idea what all this is about and who is behind it?"

"Will I get in trouble?"

"Not with us, especially if you co-operate."

"Can I have a break? I would like some coffee and some food. I haven't eaten much today."

"Yes, of course. Let me go and arrange it for you. We will take half an hour, and then we'll be back. I hope you will give us the information we are looking for."

Chapter Forty

"Staunton", he said as he picked up the phone.

"Oh, hi, Liam, this is Kevin from forensics. Someone dropped off a red petrol can for us to examine. We've given it as good going over now. There were quite a few prints from Gerry McGroarty on it, but there was another set that we retrieved from under the handle, too. I've run them through the database, but there's nothing."

"Hi, Kevin. Can you tell me anything at all about the mystery prints?"

"As in?"

"As in, do you think they are from a man or a woman? Are they from the left or right hand? You know, that sort of thing."

"Funny you should ask that. We are trialling a new test that helps to determine the gender of a fingerprint. Women's sweat has a much higher level of amino acids than men's, so we can use a control to determine the sex of the finger. It's not a hundred percent watertight, but it's a good indicator. And, of course, we have the Bayes test as well." Molloy said.

"And you're telling me all this gobbledygook because?" Staunton said.

"The Bayes test looks at the density of the ridges in a fingerprint sample. Women have a greater density of ridges than men, and in the sample, we looked at, the density was only nine per twenty-five square millimetres, so that's another indication that it was a man's print."

"So, our mystery person is a male. Thanks. You could have just said that at the start, Kevin. But it's good to know, in any case."

"OK, Mr Grumpy. What has you in such foul humour, Liam?"

"Sorry, Kevin. You wouldn't believe me if I told you. I'll pass on the info. Cheers."

* * *

Half an hour later, when Hanna Babinec was fed and watered, O'Shea and Maguire went into the interview room to continue questioning her. O'Shea opened the proceedings.

"Well, Hanna. Are you feeling better now?"

"Yes, thank you."

"Are you ready to talk openly and honestly with us then?" O'Shea said.

"I will only talk to Liam. Bring him here, and I will tell you what you need to know," Hanna said.

O'Shea looked at Maguire and shrugged. She acknowledged the gesture.

"OK, Hanna. Sergeant Maguire will go and get Detective Garda Staunton, but we will be here at all times, too. Is that understood?" O'Shea said.

Babinec just grunted and looked away.

When Maguire had left the room to go and get Liam Staunton, O'Shea studied Hanna Babinec without speaking. She really was unusually beautiful. He could easily understand how Staunton, and probably many other men, had fallen under her spell. His thoughts were interrupted when Maguire and Staunton came into the room.

As soon as Hanna Babinec saw Staunton, her eyes lit up. She smiled warmly at him as he took his seat alongside his colleagues at the other side of the table.

Maguire recited the necessary speech for the recording device that was now running again, and said, "Right, Hanna. Now that we are all here," she said, glancing sideways at Liam Staunton, "let's get on with it. Tell us what you know."

Babinec leaned forward, her elbows on the table, before she spoke.

"I'm not sure how much you know already," she said rather hesitantly, "so I'll start at the beginning. It all began about two and a half years ago. Alena was here on holidays, staying at the caravan site owned by Gerry McGroarty. She had been working hard at home, and heard that Ireland, and Westport in particular, was a good place to relax, so she came here for just a week, thinking she would be able to leave her work as an escort behind her. During her stay, McGroarty was very attentive, and after a few days, they ended up having sex. He paid her well, and she told me that afterwards, he started talking to her about an idea that he had thought up. He asked if she knew any other girls that might be interested in coming to Westport from time to time to offer their services locally. He said he could arrange the accommodation, and he would take a portion of the money that they earned in the form of rent."

The Gardaí could hardly believe what Hanna was saying, but they encouraged her to continue.

"So, Alena contacted a number of us, and we set up a kind of rota. We each came here for three or four weeks at a time, staying in the apartments owned by McGroarty or his wife. It was very profitable. There is a big demand here in the town for our services, and we did well from it."

O'Shea interrupted Hanna's flow.

"Are you saying, Hanna, that Mrs McGroarty is involved in this arrangement?"

"Oh, yes, of course. In fact, I think she is the main person behind it all. Most of our dealings are with her. She's not very nice."

"I see," O'Shea went on, "so what happened to Maria Hyka? Was she one of you too?"

"No. Not at all. Somehow, the word got out to one of the Albanian gangs that run lots of girls in all the big cities in Europe, and they wanted to see if they could muscle in on what we were doing. They sent Hyka over to see how it all worked and find out how much they could make. This has happened to us before. We have been driven out of a few places by these gangs, but we are smart, and we can usually manage to keep ahead of them."

"So, how did Maria Hyka end up dead?" O'Shea asked.

"I don't know. But I know that when McGroarty found out what was happening, he was furious. He said that he would teach them a lesson. That's all I know. Next thing, Maria is found dead at the beach. We were all very sorry, and a bit frightened too, but maybe a little bit glad too that someone had stood up to the gangs."

O'Shea looked at Maguire, signalling to her that she should take over the questioning.

"Hanna, do you think it was Mr McGroarty that killed Maria?"

"I don't know. You are the detectives. You should be able to find out. Now, can I get out of here? What are our plans, Liam?"

Maguire didn't give the junior officer time to respond.

"I think you should stay here for a while, Hanna, for your own safety. We have some things to follow up on. We will come back and let you know when we are done. In the meantime, Liam, can you get Hanna to put all this down in a proper statement."

"Yes, Sarge, sure."

Maguire and O'Shea got up and left the room, leaving Hanna Babinec and Liam Staunton alone.

Chapter Forty-One

O'Shea and Maguire retreated to O'Shea's office. They both sat down, and O'Shea said, "What do you make of that, then, Deirdre?"

"Truth is stranger than fiction, or so they say! How come we never got a whiff of any of this going on? God knows, the place is small enough. You would think it would be impossible to keep all that nonsense quiet, wouldn't you?"

"I know what you mean. But, more importantly, what are we going to do now?" O'Shea said.

"I'm not completely sure. I don't think McGroarty killed the girl, or set the fire for that matter. The film from McAllister's mobile home shows a much younger and fitter bloke making off. But McGroarty is clearly up to no good. But I imagine if we confront him head on, he might be well able to wriggle out of everything. We will have to be a bit clever with the McGroartys."

"I agree. Let's think about it for the rest of the day. What are we going to do about the two love birds downstairs?" O'Shea said.

"Maybe we should send Hanna back to Bristol, or wherever she's come from later on, and I don't think Liam should drive her to the airport either."

"I agree," O'Shea said. "Give me an hour to figure something out, and if you come up with anything, let me know."

As Maguire got up and left O'Shea's office, a germ of an idea was forming in her rather devious mind.

* * *

Hanna Babinec was sitting alone in the interview room. Staunton had left her to go about his business, and she was trying to figure out exactly what might happen next. She hadn't been charged with anything, so strictly speaking, she was free to get up and leave. But if she did that, she would have to make her own way back to Dublin, and she couldn't be sure what might happen when she got to the airport. The Irish police might have her stopped from boarding her flight now that they were aware of her actual destination.

She was trying to process all of this when Detective Sergeant Deirdre Maguire entered the room.

"Hi, Hanna. How are you getting on?" Maguire said.

"OK, thanks, but I'm just wondering what exactly happens next, Sergeant?"

"Ah. That's what I have come to talk to you about," Maguire said, sitting down. "Tell me, Hanna, did Gerry McGroarty ever take advantage of any of the girls he was, shall we say, looking after?"

"Yes, of course. He figured he was entitled. But I

managed to avoid him, though it was a close call on a few occasions. Why do you ask?"

"Excellent. So, if the opportunity arose, I imagine he would be very keen to be with you. Would you agree?"

"Yes, I suppose so. But what are you suggesting?"

Maguire went on to explain her plan to Hanna in some detail, watching carefully for a reaction from the young woman. When she had heard what Maguire had to say, she asked, "And what would be in this for me, Sergeant?"

"Well, firstly, you would be helping us to solve a particularly nasty crime, and we might be able to get you some cash from the victims of crime fund to help you out. I'm not completely sure about that, but I could have a word with DI O'Shea and see what we could do. But you should understand that if you agree, this will be the end of your visits to Westport. Not just for you, but for the rest of the girls."

Babinec shrugged.

"That's not a problem. We can easily move on to another town. It doesn't even have to be in Ireland, though I'm getting quite fond of some of your Irishmen," she said, smiling.

"It would be better if it wasn't anywhere near here, anyway, Hanna. You might not get away so lightly again."

"OK. I will do as you ask. Later this evening would be good. I'll need my phone and some place to stay," Babinec said.

"That's not a problem. I'll book you into The Westport Arms for the night. Thanks, Hanna."

* * *

Maguire found O'Shea in his office. She told him of her plan involving Hanna Babinec and watched as his eyes grew wide, and he listened intently to her.

"Jesus, Deirdre, do you not think you are playing with fire? That could easily be interpreted as entrapment, and McGroarty could take us to the cleaners," O'Shea said when she had finished laying out her idea.

"Yes, but you're not getting it, sir. I don't intend to charge McGroarty with paying for sex. I just want to use it as a lever to get him to tell us what happened. If it goes the way I think it will, he'll be scared shitless that his reputation will be destroyed, not to mention what his wife might do to him. And as you know, he could face up to five years in prison under our new laws if he was convicted, so that should loosen his tongue a bit, don't you think?"

"Bloody hell, Deirdre. It's very high risk. If it comes unstuck, both of us will be for the high jump, and God knows what the boss would have to say about it. But I see where you're coming from. What about if you keep me right out of it? This conversation never happened, and if you get into difficulties, I might just be able to jump in and help you sort it out. But only if I haven't been involved. Is that understood?"

"Yes, boss. Now, I'd better go and get a few things sorted."

Chapter Forty-Two

Maguire was busy. She had telephoned The Westport Arms and booked Hanna Babinec in for the night. She told the receptionist that the Gardaí would pay the bill for the woman, and that she should be afforded every comfort, including an evening meal, if required.

Then she had gone looking for Liam Staunton who she found brewing a cup of coffee in the little kitchenette at the back of the open plan.

"Hi, Liam. I want you to do something for me. Could you nip out to that Chinese phone shop and get a few bits and pieces for me? I want three of those very small cameras, you know, the ones. I think they call them spy cameras. Get them back here and make sure they are charged up, and they will last for two to three hours. Then, I want you to take Hanna around to The Westport Arms and check her in. Take the three cameras up to her room, and fix them up so that they record whatever is going on in the room. Make sure they are well hidden and can't be seen. OK?"

"Yes, OK, boss. What's the story?"

"Don't worry about it, Liam. Just make sure you don't mess around with Hanna. Just set the room up as I instructed and then come back here. Then in the morning, I want you to go back to the hotel and collect the cameras and bring them back here. And for heaven's sake, don't get caught. OK?"

"Yes, OK, boss. Does Hanna know that the cameras are being installed?" Staunton said.

"Don't you worry about that, Liam. I'll be briefing Hanna fully before nightfall. Just do what I have asked and then get yourself back here. You can't be anywhere near the place from about six o'clock onwards. Is that understood?" Maguire said.

"Yes, OK, but I wish you'd tell me what's going on. Don't you trust me?"

"It's not a question of trust, Liam. This particular operation is very tricky. If it doesn't go well, I could be in real trouble, and I don't want to drag anyone else into it. Trust me. It's better this way."

"Oh. OK then. I'd better get going."

* * *

While Staunton was out shopping, Maguire went back down to the room where Hanna Babinec was seated on her own.

"OK, Hanna. Now, it's time for you to play your part. Are you sure you know what to do?"

"Yes, of course," she said, taking her mobile phone out from her handbag and locating the number before pressing the call button. She let the phone ring for a few seconds, and then it was answered.

"Hello, Gerry. This is Hanna."

Maguire was amazed at the tone that Hanna used for the call. She had put on a sultry voice, and it was almost as if she was going right into the phone to talk to McGroarty. The phone was on speaker, so Maguire could hear both sides of the conversation.

"Hi Hanna, love. Where are you calling from?"

"I'm right here in Westport, Gerry. I came across it for the weekend. I'd love to see you if you can manage it."

McGroarty was silent for a moment as he processed the situation.

"Hmm .. OK. I'd like that too. Where are you staying? You're not in your old apartment, are you?"

"No. I'm staying at The Westport Arms. Do you think you could come around at about seven?"

"I guess so. Do you think that would be OK?"

"Yes. Of course. I'll text you the room number as soon as I've checked in, and then you can come straight up. We can have an hour or so."

"Yes, OK, sounds like fun."

"But, Gerry, I'll have to ask you to pay for the time you spend with me. Will that be OK?"

"Yes, of course," McGroarty said, "how much will it be?"

"For you, just a hundred. But it will be well worth it, Gerry; you know I know how to please you."

McGroarty gave a little chuckle.

"Great, Hanna. I'll be there. I'm looking forward to it."

"See you later, my love." She finished the call.

"Well done, Hanna. I don't think he suspects a thing.

Now, just remember when he arrives, you ask him for the money up front, and make it clear to him that he is paying for sex. You'll find the right words, I am sure," Maguire said.

"And what will happen then?"

"As soon as he has handed over the cash, we will come into the room and arrest him. That way, you won't have to do anything with him. We may have to pretend to detain you as well, but it will be just for show. We won't take you away with us. Then, your evening is your own. I'll call around tomorrow morning, and we can have breakfast together. We'll get you back to the airport," Maguire said.

"What about my money?"

"That will take a few days for me to organise, Hanna. But if you leave me your bank details, I'll arrange it next week and send it to you."

Hanna thought for a moment.

"Can I trust you?"

"Of course you can. I'm a police officer!"

* * *

An hour later, Maguire, Babinec, and Staunton were in room five at The Westport Arms. Babinec was unpacking the few things she had brought with her in anticipation of a passionate weekend with Liam Staunton, while Maguire examined the location of the three cameras that had been hidden around the room.

"OK, let's get out of here, Liam; leave Hanna to make herself respectable for her guest. Don't worry, Hanna, this will soon be over, and thank you for your cooperation."

Babinec just nodded.

When they were outside, Maguire said to Staunton, "Let's rendezvous at around 6:30. I'll park here on the street opposite the hotel, and we can look out for your man arriving. Give him a few minutes to get upstairs and negotiate the financials with herself, and then we'll barge in and arrest him."

"Are you going to charge him? If you do, that will involve Hanna too, won't it?" Staunton said.

"Don't worry about it, Liam. I have it all under control."

Chapter Forty-Three

Maguire and Staunton were seated in Maguire's car as arranged, waiting for Gerry McGroarty to arrive. Just after 7pm, McGroarty came walking briskly down the street. He had brushed up pretty well. He was dressed in a sports jacket and pale-coloured chinos, with a mid-blue button-down shirt, and his hair was neatly combed.

"I bet he's doused himself with aftershave," Maguire said, smirking.

"Probably," Staunton replied.

"Let's give him five minutes or so, and then we will go in."

The time seemed to drag by, but when five minutes had elapsed, Maguire said, "Right, Liam. Action stations. You know the drill."

The two detectives got out of Maguire's car and went across to the hotel. They ascended to the first floor where Babinec was lodging in room 5, and Maguire listened outside. She could hear McGroarty through the door, and when she figured that he had handed over his money to Hanna, they opened it and went in.

McGroarty was startled. He spun around to face the detectives and said loudly, "What the fuck! What the hell are you doing here?"

Hanna was playing her part, too. She slumped on the bed and started to cry, with her head in her hands.

Maguire responded quickly, holding up her warrant card.

"Mr McGroarty, I'm arresting you under the Criminal Law Sexual Offences Act 2017 for paying a woman for sexual services. You do not have to say anything, but anything you do say may be taken down and used in evidence. Do you understand?"

McGroarty looked at Hanna and said, "You little tart! I'll have you for this!"

Babinec sobbed loudly.

Maguire gestured to her colleague, "Get him out of here, Liam. Take him back to the station. I'll follow in a few minutes."

When Staunton and his quarry had left, Maguire sat on the bed beside the apparently distraught Babinec.

"Are you OK, Hanna?"

The woman looked up and smiled.

"Yes, of course," she said cheerfully, "but I hope Gerry will be held at your police station until I am away from here."

"Yes, of course. I will be questioning him tomorrow, and I'll be bringing his wife in for questioning, too. I know she is tied up with this whole thing in some way or other. Look,

I'd better go now. I'll have to take the €100 he gave you as evidence. Is that OK?"

"Yes, I suppose so. But I will need some cash to get home."

"Don't worry about that. I'll fix it up in the morning. Can we meet for breakfast at, say, 9:00am?"

"Yes, that will be fine."

When she got back to the Garda station, Maguire made sure that Gerry McGroarty had been booked in and was detained in a cell for the night. She arranged for him to be fed from the local take-away outlet. She then went upstairs to call his wife.

* * *

"Mrs McGroarty, this is Detective Sergeant Maguire here from Westport Garda station. I'm afraid to have to advise you that your husband has been arrested and is being held here in custody overnight."

"What? What are you talking about? Gerry just had to pop out to the caravan park to get some paperwork. He'll be back any minute."

"I'm afraid that's not the case, Mrs McGroarty. As I said, we have him here in custody. I'm just letting you know so that you won't be worried about him."

"But what is it that you think he has done, Sergeant?"

Maguire thought for a moment.

"I'd rather not discuss the matter over the phone. If you'd like to call into the station here at, say, 10:30am tomorrow, I can explain it all at that stage," Maguire said.

"Will he be OK? Do I need to contact a solicitor?"

"That's up to you, Mrs McGroarty, but it's not essential; your husband hasn't been charged with anything as yet. It's probably best to wait till tomorrow."

"Oh, God, this is awful. Can I see him if I come in now?"

"I'm afraid that won't be possible, Mrs McGroarty. Best if you just try and relax, and we'll see you in the morning. OK?"

"I suppose so, but I wish you'd tell me what you think he has done. He's not a bad man, Sergeant."

"Best if we leave it till the morning, Mrs McGroarty. He'll be quite safe here. We have arranged a meal for him and everything. I'll see you tomorrow."

"I suppose so," the woman said, and hung up.

Maguire then took the two €50 notes that she had placed in a see-through bag at the hotel, and placed them in the evidence lock-up. She noted that they were crisp and fresh. Presumably, McGroarty had got them from an ATM in the town on the way to meet Babinec. This was good news because there was a fair chance that his fingerprints could be recovered from them as they were virtually uncirculated.

Maguire checked with the desk sergeant that McGroarty's fingerprints had been taken again when he was booked in, and was pleased to discover that they had indeed been recorded on the system.

Maguire then went to find Liam Staunton who was at his desk updating the Garda PULSE system.

"Hi, Liam. All OK?"

"Yes, boss. Yer man is all settled in downstairs. Do you want me to help you with him tomorrow?"

"No. I'm having breakfast with Hanna tomorrow morning, and then she needs to get to Dublin airport. Would you be up to driving her, or should we put her on a bus?"

"No, it's fine. I can drive her. What time will you be finished breakfast?"

"Say 10:30am. And don't forget to collect the little cameras from her room. But no messing now, understood?"

"Yes, of course."

When Staunton was sure that Maguire had left the station for the night, he called Hanna on her mobile phone.

Chapter Forty-Four

The following morning was bright and sunny as Maguire pulled up outside The Westport Arms at just before 9am and parked. She went into the hotel and found the dining room easily on the left-hand side of the entrance hall. Hanna Babinec was seated alone at a table over by the window.

"Morning, Hanna," Maguire said.

"Good morning," Hanna replied, "you are very much on time. Have a seat."

As soon as Maguire was seated, a waitress came across and asked her what she would like for breakfast. She ordered scrambled eggs and bacon with black coffee and brown toast. She noticed Babinec was just having cereal. The waitress disappeared to get the order, and Maguire said, "So, Hanna. How was your night?"

"Very comfortable, thank you. I slept well. Did you bring me any money for my journey home?"

Maguire reached into her handbag and took out €150, handing it across the table to Babinec.

"Don't worry. It's not the same money McGroarty gave you. This is from my personal account, but I'll get it back tomorrow. Is that enough?"

"Yes, thank you. May I call you Deirdre?"

"Yes, of course."

"So, what are the arrangements for me to get to the airport? I suppose you are going to put me on a bus."

"No, we're not. I have arranged for Liam to drive you. I presume that's OK by you?" Maguire said.

"Oh. Yes, of course. That's very kind of you both. What time is he coming for me?"

"I asked him to be here at 10:30am. Will you be ready then?"

"Yes, that's fine."

Just then, the waitress arrived with Maguire's food, and the conversation was suspended while she ate.

* * *

Maguire left the hotel and went back to the Garda station when she had finished her breakfast, bidding farewell to Hanna Babinec. When she got to the station, she went directly to DI O'Shea's office, where she found him busy at his PC.

"Morning, boss. Are you ready for us to have a go at McGroarty?"

"Steady on! I haven't had my first cup of coffee yet," O'Shea said, grinning.

"Well, we need to get on with it. His wife will be here any minute shouting the odds," Maguire said.

O'Shea sighed but got up out of his chair and said, "Right. Let's do it then."

They went downstairs and asked the desk sergeant to bring McGroarty into interview room one. When the three of them were seated in the small room, Maguire recited the introduction for the recorder. She then opened the conversation.

"Mr McGroarty, you have been arrested in connection with an incident last night at The Westport Arms Hotel where you were discovered paying a young woman for sexual services. What have you to say about that?"

"You set me up, you bastards. It was she that called me and arranged the meeting. I wonder what you had to promise her to get her to do that?"

Maguire ignored the man's question and pressed on.

"Mr McGroarty, I'm sure you are aware that under the 2017 amendment to the Sexual Offences Act, you could face up to five years in prison for your actions. Furthermore, the disgrace that you will bring upon yourself and your family will make you some kind of pariah locally, not to mention what your wife may decide to do. You may well lose your business as well."

"I wasn't doing anything a lot of other men around her are doing, and you're not persecuting them, are you?"

Maguire tapped O'Shea's foot under the table, signalling that he should take over the questioning. O'Shea lent in closer to the suspect, and adapted a more conciliatory tone.

"Look, Gerry, to be honest, we aren't too bothered about you, and what's her name, Babinec is it? But we have a murder to solve, and that's what we are really after. But if you can't help us with that, then we'll press ahead with the prosecution, and it will all become very public quite quickly. Tell me, Gerry, was Maria Hyka one of your girlfriends too?"

"No, she bloody wasn't, the little tramp. She was just here to cause trouble. It's no harm that she's gone if you ask me."

"In what way was she here to cause trouble, Mr McGroarty?" O'Shea said.

McGroarty swivelled sideways in his chair.

"Look, Inspector. Things were trotting along nicely here for the last couple of years. The girls came into town, did their business, stayed for a few weeks, and left. It was all nice and peaceful, and they wouldn't have been here if there was no custom. Then, the Albanian gangs decided that they wanted to muscle in on the business. They sent Hyka to suss out the scene here - sort of an advanced guard, if you will. She was about to report back to them that they could move in and take over. The whole caper would be busted up, and they'd take over completely, and I can tell you, that would have been in no one's interests."

"You seem to know an awful lot about this operation, Mr McGroarty. Did you kill Maria Hyka?" O'Shea said.

McGroarty straightened his chair again, facing O'Shea, eye to eye.

"No, I did not. I had nothing to do with it."

"That seems unlikely to me. After all, her body was burned out close to your premises. The accelerant that was used to set the fire almost certainly came from your lock up, and your fingerprints are all over the petrol can too," O'Shea said.

"Yes. But I was nowhere near the caravan site that night. I'd been in town drinking, and I bumped into one of the girls. I went back to hers and spent the night with her. She'll tell you if you ask her."

"And which girl exactly was this?"

"Alena. She was staying at one of my wife's properties here in town."

Maguire decided to interject.

"And I presume Alena is still here in Westport, Mr McGroarty?" she said.

"You'd have to ask my wife about that. She organises the girls."

Maguire and O'Shea looked at each other in surprise.

"Are you saying that it is Mrs McGroarty that is running these women?" Maguire said.

"No. They are all freelance. Mrs McGroarty has arrangements with them. She provides them with accommodation and helps them out with some of the stuff on the internet and the bookings like, you know, the kind of thing."

O'Shea gestured to Maguire to leave the room, and she understood what he was asking of her.

Chapter Forty-Five

Maguire found Mrs McGroarty sitting patiently in the front office of the station. She had been provided with a cup of tea, and seemed quite relaxed. When Maguire approached, she stood up and said, "When can I see my husband?"

"We are still interviewing him, Mrs McGroarty. But while the inspector is finishing up with him, I wonder if we could have a little chat?"

The woman looked a little nervous but agreed, and they both made their way to the second interview room just along the corridor.

"Take a seat, Mrs McGroarty," Maguire said, sitting down herself at the other side of the table.

"Your husband has been telling us about the escort girls that are working here in the town from time to time. What do you know of this business?"

McGroarty shuffled uneasily in her seat.

"What has he told you?" she said.

"I'd like to hear it from you, please."

"I just help them with somewhere to stay, that's all. They don't like to use hotels. There's not enough privacy."

"But you know what line of business the girls are in, don't you?"

"What they do in their own time is their business, Sergeant. I don't pry into their personal affairs."

"But you do know what they are doing, don't you? And, of course, you charge them rent?"

"Naturally. I'm not a charity! They pay a fair rent, no more."

"Do you assist them in other ways at all?" Maguire said.

"Such as?"

"Such as setting up their internet adverts. Making bookings for them, that sort of thing."

Mrs McGroarty shuffled a little more in her chair.

"Sometimes, I do give them a hand with some of that stuff if they need it. It's not illegal to help someone with their computer, is it?"

"What do you know of Maria Hyka, Mrs McGroarty?"

"That little tramp. I know she was trouble, that's what."

"In what way was she trouble?"

"She came here to take over our business. Everything was going along nicely and smoothly till she arrived. She put the fear of God into the girls. She wanted her lot to take over."

"And what do you know of her death, Mrs McGroarty."

McGroarty remained silent for quite some time before saying, "I think I would like to have a solicitor now, please."

* * *

O'Shea and Maguire got together again while they were waiting for Mrs McGroarty's solicitor to turn up. The compared notes about the two interviews, and when O'Shea heard about what Mrs McGroarty had revealed, he said, "Cripes! Reading between the lines, I'd say the two of them saw Hyka off, wouldn't you?"

"Yes, but he says he has an alibi, and anyway, we can tell from the videos that it wasn't him that set the fire in the car. And I can't see the Mrs committing a brutal murder, can you?"

"I don't know. I guess it depends on how much they had to lose. Let's pull both of their bank records and see how much they have been making from all of this," O'Shea said.

"I bet it's all in cash somewhere. But you're right. We need to check. I'll get someone working on it."

* * *

The duty solicitor arrived almost an hour later and asked for half an hour to confer with his client. Ronan Joyce was a man in his forties that Maguire recognised from one of the local firms. He stood about five foot eight inches tall and was dressed in a rather ill-fitting navy suit with a white shirt and a dark tie which was loose around his collar. His brown shoes were not very clean.

After the interval allowed for conference, O'Shea and Maguire went back downstairs to continue the interview with Mrs McGroarty.

O'Shea was the first to speak.

"Mrs McGroarty, when my colleague here asked you what you knew of the death of Maria Hyka, you refused to answer and requested a solicitor. So, now I'd like to ask you again, what do you know of the death of Maria Hyka?"

"I didn't kill her."

"OK, but do you know who did?"

McGroarty looked at her solicitor, who nodded imperceptibly.

"It was probably Oisín Boyd. He's from the North of Ireland. He does a bit of work for Gerry from time to time at the site. It's all casual, you understand," Mrs McGroarty said.

"And why would you think that, Mrs McGroarty?" O'Shea said.

McGroarty looked at Joyce again, but there was no obvious response this time.

"I asked him to rough her up a bit, that's all. I definitely didn't ask him to bump her off. I just wanted to scare her so that she would leave, and not come back."

"And did you pay this Oisín Boyd to rough up the woman?"

"We paid Boyd for his work around the place."

"How much, and when did you pay him last?"

"I don't know. You'd need to ask Gerry about that. He looked after the money."

"And where exactly is this Oisín Boyd now, Mrs McGroarty?" O'Shea said.

"I dunno. He took off. I think he was scared. He probably didn't mean to kill her, but he had a bit of a temper."

"Do you have an address for this Boyd chap?"

"No. Gerry used to let him stay at the site in one of the empty caravans now and then. I don't think he had a permanent address. God knows where he is now. I certainly don't."

O'Shea tapped his colleague's foot under the table, and Maguire left the room to put out an all-points bulletin for Oisín Boyd, which would include the North of Ireland. He continued the interview on his own.

"I need to know exactly what you said to this Boyd character when you were asking him to deal with Maria Hyka, Mrs McGroarty."

She looked once again at her solicitor, but this time, he shook his head slightly from side to side.

"No comment."

O'Shea sighed and sat back in his chair with his arms spread wide.

"Very well. We'll pause this for now. I'll be back in a while."

Joyce spoke up.

"Does this mean you are releasing my client, Inspector?"

"No, Mr Joyce, it does not. As I said, I'll be back shortly."

Chapter Forty-Six

O'Shea and Maguire retreated to O'Shea's office. The inspector wasn't in a very cheery mood.

"So, where the hell does this leave us, Deirdre?" he said.

"OK. Let's look at it objectively. We can probably do Mr Mac for conspiracy to commit assault under the Offences Against The Person Act, but he'd probably get off with probation, and our proof is very thin. If we could locate Boyd, that would be much better. He'd probably do a deal to save his sorry ass and land the McGroartys right in it," Maguire said.

"What about the prostitutes?"

"I doubt if we can do much about that. The penalties are stupidly low in any case, and we could find that his lordship, the judge has been a frequent customer in any case. No. Our best bet is to catch Boyd and put him under pressure. We might get Gerry Mac for conspiracy to murder then, and that would see him put away for a good spell. We could also put the frighteners on Mrs Mac, so that she closes down her operation."

"And leaves the business to the Albanian gangs, no doubt," O'Shea said.

"I'm not so sure. After what happened to Maria Hyka, they may be reluctant to set up shop around here, at least for a while. And we could keep a good watch for anything like that and nip it in the bud. We could keep an eye on the internet and pounce if we see anyone offering their services in these parts," Maguire said.

"Hmm .. I suppose you're right."

O'Shea's desk phone sprang to life.

"Inspector O'Shea," he said, answering the thing.

"Oh, hello, Inspector. It's Jim Kenny here from Kennys Karz. I just thought I'd give you a call. That lad that bought the old black Avensis from me a while back was in again. He bought another car, and paid in cash. He drove off in it about half an hour ago."

"I see. Have you got the details of the car you sold him there?"

"Sure, of course, I have. It's a blue diesel VW Passat with an automatic gearbox. A very unusual car, if I may say so, and in very good nick for its age."

"I'm sure," O'Shea said, rolling his eyes to heaven, "what about the registration number, Mr Kenny."

"Oh, yes, right. It's 07LD75667."

O'Shea scribbled the details and the number down on a piece of paper and handed it to Maguire, gesturing for her to go off and get busy.

"Did he give you his name this time, Mr Kenny?"

"Oh, I made sure he did. I have to register the change of

ownership with the Department. He calls himself Oisín Boyd. But he didn't give me an address before you ask."

"Thanks. That's very helpful."

"Always happy to help the Guards, Inspector. Bye now."

O'Shea hung up and followed Maguire out into the open plan, where he found her sitting beside Liam Staunton at his PC. He had arrived back from Dublin where he left Hanna Babinec at the airport.

"Hi, Liam. Did everything go ok at the airport? Are we sure that woman has actually left?" O'Shea said.

"Oh, yes, boss. She's gone OK, and I don't think she'll be back," Staunton said somewhat regretfully.

"Good. Have you put out the details of Boyd and his car?"

"Yes. Have you any idea where he is headed?" O'Shea said.

"No, none. But since we got the ANPR kit in the road policing vehicles, he may be easy enough to spot."

"Let's hope so, Liam, let's hope so. Deirdre, can we finish our conversation about the two downstairs in my office?"

"Yes, of course," Maguire said.

Back in O'Shea's office, Maguire asked her boss what he was planning for the two suspects.

"Let's stick our necks out a bit here, Deirdre. It's a tad risky, but I'm not having these two going around making a mockery of the law and getting away with it. Charge Gerry with conspiracy to murder, and Mrs with brothel keeping and trafficking. That should keep them quiet for a while. They'll get bail, but so what? And once they are all lawyered up, we can do a deal for lesser charges if we can't nab Boyd," O'Shea said.

"Do you want to run it past the Super, sir?" Maguire said.

"No, I bloody don't. He'll only tell me not to do it, so the less he knows about it, the better for now."

"Fair enough. I'll go and get on with it then."

"Thanks."

* * *

Oisín Boyd was keen to get a good long way away from Westport as fast as he could. He was originally from Northern Ireland, where he had been involved with the subversives, but only on the periphery of their activities. He figured things had probably quietened down enough for him to return to his old patch in any case, and he could lie low there until an opportunity arose for him to get away to England or maybe even further afield.

The old car he had bought from Kenny was surprisingly agile. It was comfortable too, although there was a distinctive hum from the engine, but it wasn't unpleasant. He planned to drive on past Donegal Town, and then turn eastwards at Ballybofey, and cross into the North at Lifford, and use the small narrow roads to take him all the way to his destination on the outskirts of Ballymena.

When he got last Donegal Town, the N15 was straight and wide, and there was very little traffic, and in a relaxed frame of mind, he allowed the speed in the old Volkswagen to build up until he was doing well over the speed limit.

Parked in an entrance to a field, almost completely out

of sight, two Gardaí in a brightly coloured squad car were lying in wait for just such an opportunity. When Boyd went past them, clocking 130kph, they pulled out and gave chase. The caught up with him two kilometres further on, and used their blue lights to pull him over to the hard shoulder. As they came to a halt, the on-board ANPR identified the vehicle as having no insurance.

The two Gardaí got out of their car. One of them approached the driver's door, while the other called back to base to get more details on the car and its driver. When the first uniformed officer was standing abreast of the driver's window, Boyd pressed the button and lowered the glass.

"Good afternoon, sir. Do you know why you have been stopped?" he said.

"No, Guard. What's the problem?" Boyd said.

"May I see your driver's license please, sir?"

"Eh, I'm sorry, Guard, I don't have it on me."

"I see. I'm sure you realise it is an offence not to have your license available for inspection at the roadside. What's your name?" the Guard said, a little less politely.

"Oisín Boyd. Look, I'm sorry about the license. I can produce it tomorrow at a Garda station for you. Is that OK?"

"Not really. And another thing. We clocked you driving well in excess of the speed limit back there, and our system tells us that you have no insurance on the vehicle. So, I'm afraid I'm going to have to ask you to step out of the car and give me the key."

"Ah, shit Guard, give me a break. I only just bought the car earlier today. I'll get it insured tomorrow if you just let me go."

"Sorry, Mr Boyd. I can't do that. You'll have to come with us in the squad car, and your vehicle will be seized. We'll take you back to the station, where you will be charged under the Road Traffic Act for speeding and driving without insurance. I see the tax has expired too, and I don't see a current NCT disc in the windscreen either, so there will be quite a few offences to take into consideration."

Boyd said nothing, but seeing that he was outnumbered, he followed the officer's instructions, sitting into the back of the squad car while a tow truck was summoned to impound the old Volkswagen.

Chapter Forty-Seven

As soon as Boyd arrived at the Garda station on Quay Street in Donegal Town and his details were being entered into the system, the notice that he was being sought popped up on the desk sergeant's computer. The man telephoned Westport and spoke to a delighted Detective Sergeant Maguire.

"That's terrific news. Thanks very much Sergeant. Do you think you could leave him back down with us, or would you prefer if we came and collected him?" Maguire said to the sergeant in charge.

"Ah, we'll drop him down to you. The lads will enjoy the trip. It's a grand fine day for a drive."

"Excellent. Many thanks again," Maguire said.

She then went and broke the good news to her boss, who was equally pleased with the new development.

"Fantastic, Deirdre. Maybe we're getting somewhere at last with this whole mess. What about the McGroartys?"

"I packed them off home on bail pending further enquiries. They were feeling very sorry for themselves, both blaming each other for the mess that they had created. I'd say the next time we see them, they'll be all lawyered up."

"A don't worry. Now that we have Boyd, things will swing in our direction. Can you hang on till he gets here?"

"Yes, sure. I wouldn't miss it for the world."

* * *

It was early evening when Oisín Boyd was delivered to Westport Garda station by the officers from Donegal. Boyd was again booked in, and his fingerprints taken before he was ushered away to a cell to contemplate his dilemma. The two Gardaí that had driven down with him were plied with tea and sandwiches and thanked profusely before setting off again for the two-hour drive back to base.

O'Shea and Maguire got together, and they both went downstairs to interview their suspect.

"Well, Oisín, what a right old mess you've managed to create for yourself. And I'm not talking about a few motoring offences," O'Shea said, opening proceedings.

"I don't know what you mean," Boyd said gruffly.

"Well, let me help you with that. We're investigating the brutal murder of a young woman here in Westport, who was not only brutally attacked and killed, but was then driven to a remote location and set on fire. Sound familiar?"

"I don't know what you're talking about."

"I'm talking about murder, Mr Boyd. Brutal, savage murder. And I think, we have our man, wouldn't you agree Sergeant Maguire?"

"Looks like it to me, boss. Let's see now. We have a statement from the man who sold you the Toyota Avensis in which the body was found. We have the petrol can that contained the accelerant used to burn the girl's body with your fingerprint on it. And, of course, we have McGroarty's statement implicating you. How much did they pay you to see off Maria Hyka, Oisín?"

"No comment."

O'Shea came back at the young man.

"I'm afraid no comment won't do this time, Oisín. You're going down for murder. That's a life sentence in these parts, and I can just imagine how welcome you will be in Limerick jail given your previous history."

"I think I need a lawyer," Boyd said.

"I think you do. But that will have to wait till tomorrow, I'm afraid, so I hope you'll be nice and comfortable in one of our cells till the morning," O'Shea said, looking at Maguire and gesturing that the interview was over for now.

Once outside the interview room, O'Shea said that he was going to go and find the superintendent and bring him up to speed. Luckily, the senior man hadn't left for the day.

* * *

O'Shea explained the entire saga to his boss, Superintendent O'Connell, over a cup of tea in the senior man's spacious office. O'Connell listened intently to the sorry tale, and then said, "All right, Martin. This is how I see it. You have this Boyd fella more or less banged to rights. It was obviously he who bumped off this Hyka woman, and while he will go down for murder, he may actually have done us all a favour. The McGroartys are another matter. I wouldn't like the press to get hold of the notion that Westport is crawling with hookers and all sorts. And if we pursue that line, we never know what, or who might be uncovered as being involved. Can you not get them on some minor charge that doesn't involve sex workers and leave it at that?"

"Hmm .. I suppose the old reliable tax evasion might work. I doubt that they pay tax on all of their rent receipts, and the properties are probably not registered with the PTRB either. It will take a few months to sort all that out, but we could bring some sort of charge under that heading then, I suppose. But do you not think, sir, that they are responsible for the woman's death?" O'Shea said.

"Maybe they are. But you'll never prove that McGroarty instructed Boyd to actually kill her. They'll both say that he was told just to rough her up a bit. That way, Boyd can plead manslaughter. You might get McGroarty on conspiracy to cause actual bodily harm, but if you do that, the whole lot will come out, and I really don't think that would be in our best interests. Can you keep Maguire on-side?"

"She won't like it any more than I do, sir. But I'll be able to manage her all right."

"Good man, Martin. I knew I could rely on you to do the right thing."

On the way back downstairs, O'Shea wondered if perhaps O'Connell or some of his cronies from the golf club might not have been customers of Maria, Elena, or even Hanna, but he sure as hell wasn't going to ask.

Chapter Forty-Eight

The following morning, Boyd was interviewed again, this time in the company of the duty solicitor.

The interview went back and forth, with quite a bit of 'no comment' from the young man. But the Gardaí had all the evidence that they needed to put Boyd well and truly in the frame. Eventually, he decided to open up, hoping to avoid a murder charge.

"It was all down to Gerry McGroarty, you see. He wanted Hyka dealt with. She was a threat to the nice little business he had going with Mrs. So, he asked me to rough her up and scare her half to death so that she would disappear and take a clear message back to the gangmaster that Westport was not up for grabs. I arranged a date with her up at Tober Hill, but instead of having sex with her, I whacked her with a hammer. I didn't mean to kill her, honest. She just turned as I was wielding the thing, and it caught her on the side of the head. I was just planning on breaking her nose."

"Charming," O'Shea said.

"So, I didn't mean to kill her, just send a message. When I saw she was dead, I panicked. I didn't know what to do. So, I bundled her into the old car and drove her down to the caravan site. I knew McGroarty had petrol in the shed, and I had a key, so I got the fuel and set the car on fire. I thought you lot would think that it was a punter that had pissed her off, and they had a fight. To be honest, I didn't care once I could get away."

O'Shea looked at Maguire briefly, who took over the questioning.

"How much did McGroarty pay you to attack the girl, Oisín?" Maguire asked.

"Two grand. He makes loads of money from the girls. He keeps it all in cash down at the caravan site."

"And where did you hide out all this time?"

"I stayed in one of the empty mobile homes. McGroarty told me to lie low, and then he'd give me more money to buy a car and bugger off. I'd have got clean away if those two cops up in Donegal hadn't been looking for someone to victimise," Boyd said.

The solicitor hid his face in his hands.

O'Shea was back on the case.

"OK, Oisín. Here's the deal. You plead guilty to manslaughter, and say nothing to anybody about any of the other stuff. Don't mention escort girls or anything to anyone. Leave that for us to deal with. You'll get seven or eight years, and if you behave, you'll be out in five."

The solicitor saw an opportunity and interjected.

"Could not call it aggravated assault, Inspector? That

would probably mean that Oisín would only get a total of five years."

"No, we couldn't. And, what's more, if your client doesn't stick to these arrangements, I'll call a mis trial and re-arrest him for murder. Is that understood?"

The solicitor whispered behind his hand to his client, before saying, "Very well. Manslaughter it is, and no mention of any of the other stuff. Will you ask the judge to take his cooperation into account, Inspector?"

"Don't push it, sir. He's doing pretty well as it is."

* * *

Boyd was brought to court and charged with manslaughter. As predicted, he was given a seven-year sentence with the last two years suspended on the basis that he had pleaded guilty. He made no mention of any of the other business. He was eventually freed after just three years and moved to the UK.

Maguire and O'Shea worked with the Criminal Assets Bureau who managed to recover over €30,000 from the stash that Boyd had told them about at the caravan park. The CAB tried to confiscate Mrs McGroarty's apartments, but were not successful.

Hanna went back to Bristol. She continued her career as an escort girl for several years as long as her good looks held up. She didn't return to Ireland, but Liam Staunton made a few trips to see her, unbeknownst to the Gardaí.

The caravan park continued to do well in the summer months. Mrs McGroarty found another enterprise. She opened a small café in Westport, which did well. Maguire visited the place a few times, and wasn't surprised to find that it was staffed by a few very attractive Eastern European girls. Maguire often wondered if serving coffee and pastries was their only occupation.

Printed in Great Britain
by Amazon

60824787R00160